THE DÆMONS
OF DEVIL'S END

THE DÆMONS
OF DEVIL'S END

Edited by
SAM STONE

First published in 2017 by Telos Publishing Ltd

Telos Publishing values feedback. If you have any comments about this book please email

feedback@telos.co.uk

The Dæmons of Devil's End © 2017, Telos Publishing

Edited By Sam Stone

Foreword © 2017, Damaris Hayman
The Inheritance, Prologue, Epilogue © 2017, Sam Stone
Half Light © 2017, Suzanne Barbieri
The Cat Who Walked Through Worlds © 2017, Debbie Bennett
The Poppet © 2017, Jan Edwards
Dæmos Returns © 2017, David J Howe
Hawthorne Blood © 2017, Raven Dane
Afterword © 2017, Keith Barnfather
Dossier © 2017, Andrew-Mark Thompson

ISBN: 978-1-84583-970-3

Cover Art: © 2017, Matt Niblock
Main Photograph © 2017, Ian Burgess

CONTENTS

FOREWORD
Damaris Hayman

As an actress, you're often asked to play roles for stage or screen, and for the most part they are forgotten within a week of you completing the work. It's rare that an actor gets to play something which has longevity. But when the director, Christopher Barry, cast me as Olive Hawthorne in a 1971 *Doctor Who* story called *The Dæmons*, I think the response to it took everyone by surprise.

I remember the filming down in the little village of Aldbourne well. We had rehearsed the scenes to be filmed for a fortnight in London before going to Wiltshire and this was not a happy time for me. I knew exactly who Olive Hawthorne was – after all, we had a lot in common. But Christopher had other ideas. So rehearsals were a struggle for me, between trying to give the director what he wanted, and doing what I knew to be right. Mercifully, Ronnie Marsh, the Head of Serials, who I'd worked with in the days when he was an actor, came to one of the final rehearsals and apparently said to Christopher, Let her alone she knows what she's doing. After that, all in the garden was lovely, and at the end of the production Christopher said to me, 'You were right and I was wrong'. Precious few directors would be man enough to do that.

Our first few days at Aldbourne were unseasonably hot for April, so when it came to the scene of opening the Barrow, artificial snow and a tempest had to be provided. The next day the weather broke and there was a heavy snowfall which had to be cleared away for that day's filming. Mercifully it did not last long. It was a happy time, we all liked each other and enjoyed playing word games during the many waits. The favourite consisted of one person thinking of a character and then the others replying to cryptic questions as to who the character was. Nick Courtney had defeated Jon Pertwee over this, but on another day I got it! Nick had chosen Metternich (a German diplomat and statesman from the early 1800s), and the question I asked was: 'Was a very elaborate cake named after you?' ... and of course it was. Jon was so pleased he bought me a drink on the strength of it.

What I don't think anyone expected was how well received that story would be. I receive fan mail – every actor does – but those five episodes of *Doctor Who* have generated more mail than anything else I have ever done! And Olive Hawthorne was a part which meant a great deal to me! I started acting professionally in 1949 but had been acting and performing from about the age of six. I had a good career under my belt come 1971. There were numerous plays on television, Comedy Playhouse roles, appearances in *Emergency Ward 10* and *Steptoe and Son*, *Z-Cars*, *Armchair Theatre*, *Citizen James*, *Hugh and I*, *Hancock's* and a serial, *Ours Is A Nice House* starring Thora Hird, and *Ann Veronica* which was directed by Christopher Barry ... quite a respectable CV even if I do say so myself. It was then Christopher who offered me the part of Olive Hawthorne, who seemed to have it all – a White Witch, something of a do-gooder, but also an element of the comedic, which is important in a drama dealing with devils from another world, to leaven the terror, and to allow watching children to perhaps not be quite so scared as they otherwise might be.

What I certainly didn't expect was to be contacted by Keith Barnfather in 2010 and asked if I would reprise my character of Olive for a new drama ... something which looked back at the life of the character and postulated what other terrors she might have faced ... Of course I agreed at once, and Keith assembled a fine script and a pantheon of writers to give life to my fictional memories, and in one case an actual memory.

This book is the result of all those labours – it takes the original scripts and presents them as a narrative; the ongoing story of Olive and her struggles with evil and the unknown. I hope you enjoy reading it, as I enjoyed bringing life to Olive all those years ago, and then revisiting her for Keith's production, finally released at the end of 2017.

Go in peace

Damaris Hayman,
September 2017

PROLOGUE
Sam Stone

It's a still night. The kind of evening where I can feel something brewing. I'm alone in my cottage, surrounded by the things I hold dear. My grimoire is on my lap, but beside me, on a small table, is my crystal ball, my tarot cards, an old, faded photograph of my beloved friend Rhadamanthus and a poppet doll. Around my neck is an important amulet: an ankh on a gold chain. I never remove it but one day hope to pass it on to the right person.

These are the trappings of my craft. You see, my name is Olive Hawthorne and I am a witch, white of course ... or at least that is what I tell those who ask ...

It's almost time ...

Strange how my life has led to this moment. And you, my dear, old friend, my grimoire. You have been by my side all of this time. You have guided me with the wisdom of the words you hold. You have made me the powerful being that I have become. Shaped me into the protector that I needed to be. You have been my only mentor.

What is going to happen to you when I'm gone? The worry of you falling into the wrong hands is the only fear I feel for my impending fate. But, I need to be calm. Everything works out in the end, I know that. Though every time I look into my crystal ball all I can see is the final day. Oh not how it happens, you never see that. Just that it will and there is nothing I can do.

Even though I'm ready to go, I'm not yet ready to let go ... But, I know I have served my purpose: I've protected my little village of Devil's End. This has been my life's work after all, but I can't imagine how things will go on without me. You see this place ... it's a magnet to evil and there has to be a protector ...

There was a time when I wouldn't have worried about such things. I had my whole life ahead of me. Now, the grains of my existence are draining away faster than sand through fingers – and there is no one left to take over.

And that is the crux of the problem.

There was only ever me, and time was supposed to bring me an heir to the legacy, but time is no longer my friend. It is now my enemy.

I sigh in terror at the thought of my abandonment of the village. But these emotions are wasted and can serve no purpose other than to cause me distress. I call to Gaia. Hoping that the Earth mother will hear my prayer.

Please! Send me an heir to whom I can pass on this legacy!

Nothing stirs as always. No response comes to my plea. Even so, I have hope. Hope is never wasted.

I place down my grimoire and glance out of my window. Tonight I have a feeling of déjà vu. And the stillness persists, as though it is a lull before a great storm. It reminds me … but no. That night was so long ago … and there could never be another like it.

But I cannot shake the feeling. *That* night. And Poppy, dear Poppy …

And so, I remember the night when my simple childish world changed forever.

THE INHERITANCE
Sam Stone

I grew up in this very same cottage in Devil's End, the elder of twin girls. My sister Poppy and I were identical in looks but so different in our personalities that our mother often commented on it. Although we were indistinguishable in looks, Poppy always wore her hair in two neat plaits. She didn't like her hair getting into her eyes. I, on the other hand, always wore mine loose, flopping around my face and shoulders. It was a reflection on our inner temperaments. Poppy was organized, controlled in every way. She was quietly spoken and polite. I was chaos. Outspoken. Often I would forget my manners and mother would chide me for it. Mother's friends often praised Poppy for her ladylike behaviour, and rolled their eyes at my tomboyish ways. We were as chalk and cheese as two people hatched from the same egg could ever be.

It even showed in the way we kept our bedroom. I was never as neat and tidy as Poppy, though I tried to be organised – I just wasn't very good at it. My side of the bedroom was often littered with things I found. I loved nature, brought fresh flowers home weekly: but Poppy barely noticed. Nor did she notice the animal bones I found out in the woods. Small skulls, picked clean long before I found them, churned up from the soil by wild dogs, or rural foxes.

Poppy didn't mind my macabre collection, though our mother grimaced whenever she came into our room to dust. For that reason, on cleaning day, I would remove them and store them in a drawer, only to carefully replace them back on top of my chest of drawers after Mother left the room.

Poppy on the other hand had nothing on her chest of drawers, other than a bottle of *Lily of the Valley* perfume. Aunt

Georgina had given it to her on our last birthday when we turned 16. She had given me perfume too, but my scent was *Lavender*: different scents for two very different girls.

Devil's End was an interesting place to grow up: a small village, with a close-knit community. It was a safe place for young girls to be free, or so I thought in my innocent youth. I was often out roaming the village or the adjacent woods alone, while Poppy would remain at home, studiously reading, or baking with Mother. She showed no interest in my pursuits. And as for me, the only cooking I was attracted to involved herbs. The only books I read, talked about nature and natural healing medicines. You see I was fascinated with more than the world around us. I was already on my way to becoming a witch and healer, but I was unaware of it at the time.

Another difference between us was imagination. I had an overactive mind and it often caused me sleepless nights. Poppy slept the sleep of the just, whereas I was sometimes plagued with nightmares. It was irritating and unfair that I should suffer so from what Mother referred to as 'the night terrors', when Poppy never thought beyond the immediate, nor worried about the future.

Sometimes I had dreams of demons and monsters invading Devil's End. I would wake with sweat covering my brow. At such times I would sit up in bed and look across the room. I would see Poppy's shape, sleeping soundly in her bed, as the sun came up and peeked around the curtains, bringing natural light into the dull room. I would hear her gentle breathing and sigh with annoyance that I couldn't share her peaceful mindset.

'Don't you ever have nightmares?' I would ask her when she finally awoke.

'Of course not, silly!' she smiled. 'What on Earth is there to be afraid of?'

She was so calm, so serene all of the time, whereas I was so loud and boisterous and full of anxiety for some unexplained phobia. For this reason I found it difficult to settle and be composed.

'Why can't you sit still for a few moments,' Mother would

say. 'Read a book … or just talk with Poppy and me.'

'Oh Mother! It's a beautiful day outside. Nature is calling. Who wants to read some fusty old book when you have life instead? Besides I'll have much more to say at dinner this evening if I'm not at home all day.'

'I just don't know what you do with yourself, Olive,' Poppy laughed. 'I'd be bored if I didn't read.'

'I'd be bored if I stayed inside all the time!' I said.

I scooped an apple out of the fruit bowl on the kitchen table and stuffed it into my knapsack before hurrying out of the back door.

Out in the woods I pulled my sketch pad out of my knapsack and sat down on a fallen log, near a patch of white foxglove. I sketched the flowers for a while, then annotated the picture with notes on what I knew of its properties. Foxglove was dangerous in the wrong hands of course, and it wasn't a flower I would pick to bring home as an ornament. But it fascinated me, as did all of nature.

I sat and daydreamed for a while, listening to the sounds of the birds in the trees. It was only in these moments that I felt truly tranquil and when that unnameable fear would recede, giving my mind and soul the rest it needed.

When my stomach began to growl I took out the apple and ate it, before burying the core in a small clearing, where I hoped that one day another tree would emerge from it. If you take from nature, you should always give something back. This is a deep rooted belief that all witches, warlocks, shamans and wizards have always understood.

Our world was changing and soon there would be less understanding of the old ways than there had ever been, though I was yet to understand this. Even so, I felt as though I was on the brink of some revelation and after my light snack I returned to my quiet reflection. It was funny how like Poppy I became when I was alone. It was almost as if my loudness was an antidote to her quietude. Yet I was so happy sitting inaudibly when I was surrounded by trees and flowers. Nature made me feel peaceful.

This thought passed through my mind, along with a vision of Mother and Poppy finding me so silent and the thought of their surprised faces made me chuckle. Bird song burst forth as I giggled, as though they too saw the joke.

Then something very strange occurred: the woods became completely soundless. An ominous vacuity followed.

I looked around wondering at the stillness. Not even a rustle of leaves or the flight of a bird overhead could be heard. For the first time I felt completely alone in the woods, and the enormity of that thought hit me with the impact of my vivid imagination. What if there was some danger that the animals and birds understood but I did not?

There was no reason for the silence that I could see, but I stood up, swinging my knapsack up and over my shoulder.

I turned and retraced my steps back through the woods towards the outskirts of the village. Then as I reached the first cottage, the usual sounds of nature returned. I glanced across the village green and noted that there was no one around: a most unusual occurrence, especially near The Cloven Hoof tavern where some of the older retired men of the village often lingered on a warm afternoon.

I looked back over my shoulder into the woods. By then I knew that a storm was brewing. The clouds overhead had thickened, and the air was heavy and humid. We hadn't had rain for several weeks, and so a storm would be welcome, particularly by the farmers. But was this impending tempest the reason for the portentous silence?

I hurried through the village, running across the green as the first drops of rain spat from the clouds above. The sky flashed as I reached our front gate, and then the heavens opened and the rain fell in earnest. I made it inside the house before the rain could soak through my gingham dress but I was damp and cold: chilled to the bone by the sudden change of energy in the air.

'I'm so glad you made it home in time,' Mother said. 'This storm seems to have come from nowhere.'

It was certainly true that when I had left there had been

glorious sunshine.

'Strange isn't it?' I said frowning.

Mother didn't reply, she was preparing vegetables for our evening meal.

But I was left to ponder in uncharacteristic silence about the odd thunder storm because I could not recall such a quick and sudden change to such a wonderful summer's day before.

Late afternoon the storm dwindled and died, leaving the air feeling cleaner than it had.

Father came home from work at 7pm and soon afterwards mother served dinner on the kitchen table.

Poppy said grace – I never offered – and then Mother filled our plates with vegetables, roast chicken and her wonderful gravy.

I was quite hungry and so I ate all of my food and even asked for seconds that night. I ignored the surprised glances that followed. I normally had such a small appetite.

After dinner we cleared the table. Poppy washed and I dried the pots and pans.

'Did you see the storm, Daddy?' Poppy asked as Mother wiped down the table and put a pack of cards down in the centre.

Father had been returned to us some eight months earlier, when he was discharged from the army on medical grounds. He had been badly injured, and now could not use his left hand because it was paralyzed. He had been fortunate to get a job at the dairy, where he worked as the foreman. There were so few young men left in the village, as most had been drafted. Since his return the war felt like a life-time away from us. Mother had been constantly afraid when the post arrived all the time he was absent. And I recalled the day she was told he was injured. All colour had drained from her pretty face and Poppy and I had gathered her into our arms, telling her over and over that Father would be fine. Later Poppy had cried in my arms. She hadn't believed that Father would be fine, but I reassured her. I knew somehow he would be and that his return to us was a wonderful thing despite the circumstances.

Mother had been much happier once Father came home. He wasn't fit and well, and his recuperation took many months but before long we stopped noticing his twisted hand. Poppy and I had fallen into a domestic calm that was conducive to the happy childhood we otherwise had, pushing the dark reality of war as far away from our minds as was possible in that time.

And then, Father got the job, which meant that he was usually inside the dairy during the day, overseeing the production of cheese and the bottling of milk to be sent out to the local shops. It was all carefully rationed, but sometimes he brought home some whey that mother could use to bake with. His day was often uneventful but the storm had affected the dairy in a way no one could have predicted.

'Unfortunately one of the milk carts was struck by lightning as it reached the dairy. It was all hands to the deck today,' Father told us after dinner that night.

'How awful!' said Mother. 'Was anyone hurt?'

'Old farmer John was injured. He was taken to the voluntary hospital in the city. No word on how he's doing so far …'

Mother was subdued by the news. These were difficult times, but at least Devil's End wasn't a likely target for bombing. Even so, we had plans and strategies in place should the need arise. But acts of nature could be just as devastating as a bomb strike and the news that Farmer John was injured was enough to send us all into a period of contemplation.

Mother took an apple pie out of the oven and left it to cool in the centre of the table. Then she dealt the cards to take our mind off the bad news. After we played a few games, she cut us each a small slice of the pie. There was no custard, eggs being in such short supply, but the pie was delicious nonetheless.

'Good night, Daddy,' Poppy said. 'Night, Mummy.'

She kissed both of our parents on the cheek and stifling a yawn went to bed. I wasn't as tired as she was, but soon followed.

In our room Poppy was sleeping soundly and even though I wasn't too quiet she didn't stir. I glanced over at her, momentarily annoyed and envious of her ability to sleep so easily.

It was then I noticed that she had left her amulet on the table beside her bed. It was an ankh on a long chain and had been left to us by a distant aunt. We were supposed to share it, but Poppy was drawn to the necklace and so wore it more frequently than I.

The ankh was an Egyptian symbol and it represented life. I had always seen it as a good omen. One that would protect Poppy or me should we need it. That night I felt an overwhelming urge to have the ankh around my neck and close to my heart.

I ran my hand over it, picked it up and slipped it over my head on impulse.

Then I put my candle down on my bedside table and climbed into bed. Blowing out the candle I turned over and closed my eyes.

'Poppy? *Poppy*? Did you hear that?' I called as something jolted me awake.

I was convinced I had heard something, but as Poppy continued to sleep I began to question myself. It must have been another dream …

I closed my eyes and tried to go back to sleep, but I heard the noise again. I pushed back the covers, and climbed out of bed. There was a sound coming from outside: a strange whistle on the air. I went to the window, rubbing the sleep from my eyes, and I pulled the curtain aside.

Outside a white light illuminated the garden. There was an eerie glow coming from our empty stables and I briefly recalled stories I'd heard of fairies dancing in flower circles at the bottom of gardens. This was most curious.

'*Poppy*!' I said again. 'Come and see this.'

But Poppy remained oblivious and even though I shook her, my sister refused to wake. I could smell *Lily of the Valley*, Poppy's favourite flower and the scent captured in Poppy's perfume. It was peculiarly compelling.

I looked out of the window once more and the illumination was still there.

'Blockhead!' I said, feeling somewhat exasperated again by Poppy's ability to sleep so well. 'You'd sleep through anything!'

I lit the candle and picked it up. The light gave the room a dream-like quality and I wondered if I was indeed still dreaming. I paused for a moment, giving Poppy a final, agitated glance, then I opened the bedroom door.

On the landing I could hear the usual house sounds. The creak of the wooden beams as the house cooled, the tick-tick of the grandfather clock in the hallway and the silence of its occupants sleeping. I passed my parent's bedroom pausing to listen at the door. It was obvious that they had also not been disturbed by the whistling sound, or the light outside. If there had been a noise at all, and not something I merely imagined. It occurred to me that whoever was behind it could be endangering my family and our village by this blatant light show. After all an enemy aircraft could be flying over and might see it.

I contemplated waking my parents but an inner voice warned against it. I was extremely curious about the origins of the light, and the sound, that now appeared to be music floating on the night air. Music … like the voice of an angel singing solo in a heavenly choir or one of those mythical sirens that sailors claimed to hear.

But no. Such things did not inhabit the real world.

Convinced now that this was an elaborate dream and I was somehow self-aware, I walked away from my parent's door without knocking and soon reached the top of the stairs.

In the hallway, at the bottom of the narrow staircase, I discovered that the front door was open and the mysterious light pulsated into the hall. I paused again. The night air was cool, and a breeze whipped in snuffing the candle with one hissing breath. I placed the now useless candlestick on the bureau in the hall and stood in the doorway looking out into the night with my arms wrapped around myself as I shivered. But it was more with anticipation than with cold.

The light poured in around me and I felt a gentle tingling sensation, coupled with an overwhelming urge to walk forward. All fear of catching a chill fled. I felt warm. Protected. Without looking at the time I passed the grandfather clock and walked bare-footed over the cold path and onto damp grass.

I was drawn towards the stable. Here the light was brighter and it gave off a reassuring heat that warmed my chilled limbs. The thought of the enemy seeing it was now forgotten in my desire to know who or what was responsible as I stood before the open stable door. And then, with no will of my own, I was swept over the threshold.

The stable doors closed behind me with a dull thunk. I stopped walking as the barn was so brightly illuminated that my eyes watered. I blinked and tried to see what was behind the light through slitted eyes but it only made my vision worse as my eyes and nose streamed. I could see nothing.

I heard the frightening sounds of a storm gathering again above the house and stable. I felt comforted by the light as the rainstorm began once more. Surely my parents and sister would be woken by this and come to find me?

My bleary eyes were drawn to the far side of the barn. Here the light pulsed so brightly I had to shield my eyes with my arm. Almost immediately, as if in response to my gesture, the light began to dim. It was like a gaslight being turned down and my vision was no longer impaired by it.

Thunder rattled overhead, followed by a sudden flash of lightning. I lowered my arm and found myself face to face with an old gypsy woman.

'Come, Olive,' said the woman.

'Who are you?' I asked not even registering that she knew me!

'I'm here to give you something very important,' she answered.

'This is a dream,' I said. 'Any moment I'll wake.'

The old gypsy laughed and held out a thick, leather-bound book. I stared at the book, but was, at first, too afraid to take it.

The cover was inlaid with a golden pattern that looked like

Egyptian hieroglyphics. I recognised the ankh among them and I glanced down at the necklace I wore.

'Yes,' said the gypsy, 'you see the connection. Look! The book is responding to you …'

The strange writing began to glow on the book cover and I realised that this had been the source of the light all along. This beautiful writing was the illumination I sought.

'You have Hawthorne blood in your veins,' the gypsy continued, 'and this is your birthright.'

'I don't understand. This *must* be a dream.' I rubbed my eyes and pinched my arm as hard as I could. 'Ouch!'

I felt the bruise starting up on my arm where I had nipped my skin. I wasn't asleep at all. This was real!

'There's nothing to fear,' the gypsy said and just like that I was unafraid. I knew I was completely safe with her and so I stepped closer.

'My name is Lobelia,' she said. 'I'm a witch. And I am your great aunt. The elder sister of your grandmother.'

'That's impossible,' I said.

My grandmother had died a few years earlier and she had appeared to be a very old woman at the time. The gypsy, although aged, didn't seem as old as my grandmother had been.

'Magic is a funny thing,' said Lobelia as though reading my mind. 'It will preserve you for as long as necessary. Then, you must pass on the power to another of our blood line.'

The gypsy held out the book and as if they had a will of their own my hands reached out. I grasped it and knew it belonged to me.

I explored the surface of the book with cautious fingers. It was beautiful, uneven in places, smooth in others, as though centuries of Hawthorne witches had caressed the leather with loving care, just as I did then, and had worn the leather or worked in the natural oil from their finger tips.

'What does this all mean?' I asked.

'You are descended from a long line of witches. Your purpose in life is to protect Devil's End from all evil influences.

Evil is drawn here, and this is a gateway of sorts, that could be used to unleash untold malevolence on the world.'

I didn't really understand then how true all of her warnings would turn out to be, but I believed them all the same. There was something about the sincerity of her words and the honesty in her eyes that convinced me she was telling the truth.

'Always chose the right path, Olive,' she told me. 'All witches have the potential for goodness, as well as evil. The choices you make could mean terrible sacrifices and often loneliness.'

'You mean you are a white witch?' I said.

Lobelia chuckled. 'Olive, all witches are what they are. There is no such thing as a white witch, only those who choose to do no harm.'

Then Lobelia told me who and what I really was.

Her talk of the future made me feel strong and grown up, even though at 17 I was technically already a woman.

When she had finished telling me that I was the guardian of our small village, and the importance of my role and future I had more questions than I thought there could be answers for.

'Answer me one thing,' I said as I clutched the large book to my chest. I could hardly wait to unlock its secrets in the privacy of my room but I tried to hide my urgency from Lobelia.

'Anything, child,' said the gypsy. 'Now is the time to ask me what you must.'

'If everything you say is true, why do I have such terrible nightmares?' I asked.

Lobelia smiled and stretched out a frail hand to stroke my brow.

'Dreams are sometimes memories of our ancestors. That is why they feel so real. Sometimes they hold a portent for the future. You must always listen to your dreams. And if, at sometime in the future, you experience a feeling of *déjà vu* just as you have all day today, then take heed. It is a warning of something that has already happened, that you are about to discover.'

'I don't understand,' I said.

'The future is always the past at some point in time. But when you get these feelings, take it as a sign that the outcome has not yet been determined. Whether things end well or not will be your responsibility. Especially here in Devil's End. For time does fall in its own way in some places …'

I pondered her words, hugging the book.

'This is a grimoire,' Lobelia explained. 'As you can tell, it knows it now belongs to you. And it will guide you through the coming difficult years, helping you hone your craft.'

'Everything I need to know is inside?'

Lobelia nodded. 'But also, as you move into the future, you will remember more of what we talked about on this never-ending night …'

'What do you mean?' I asked.

'We have time, Olive. All the time you need in order for you to be strong enough. When you leave this place, you will be the guardian of Devil's End. And you will carry inside you the knowledge to save the world.'

I couldn't comprehend all that she said. But the night did feel never-ending. It was as though we were frozen in a place where time stood still but we did not. It felt as though I had taken a sideways step from the world into – and this was a new concept for me to grasp – an alternative realm.

'Take this,' Lobelia said holding out an old bridle that had hung in the back of the stable for as long as I could remember. 'This was mine as a child. Hang it over the beam above your bed and hold the reins as you go to sleep.'

I asked if this meant that the nightmares would stop, and again the old woman smiled.

'For a time, yes,' she said. 'And when they return they will no longer have the power to frighten you. By then you will have the skill to interpret them, and use the warnings to make the right decisions for the future.'

I took the bridle and placed it on top of the book.

'Now, go back to bed,' Lobelia said.

'Will I see you again?' I asked.

'Not in this world, but in the next,' she said. 'But I will

always be here.' She pointed to her temple. 'I will always be inside your memory and you will still be able to call forth our conversations when you need them.'

The words on the book, and the ankh began to glow once more. Lobelia covered her eyes as though the light was too bright for her, but it no longer hurt my eyes. It was a further sign that the book recognised me as its owner.

'Leave me now,' she said. 'You must not be here when the final moment arrives.'

I did as she bade, backing out of the stable as the doors opened of their own volition once more. The light left with me, and afraid now that my family would wake and find me with the book, I willed the grimoire to go dark. It responded to my unspoken command immediately.

I entered the house, closing the front door behind me, and tripped upstairs as silently as possible while pondering Lobelia's words. What was the 'final moment'? The answer occurred to me as I reached the landing and I almost turned back. The woman was going to die! Alone. It was too horrible to imagine!

I felt an overpowering responsibility to be with her in those last seconds, but the book flashed light briefly blinding me. I paused and waited for the answer to come to me. An overwhelming sense of peace came over me. I glanced out of the window looking over the stable and knew that all was well. Lobelia was no longer there. She had gone onto another plane. I was not needed.

Back in our room I saw that Poppy still slept soundly and I decided not to try and wake her. I wanted to think things through first. I wasn't sure if she would believe my story, or even if I should show her the grimoire. Perhaps this was a question I should have asked Lobelia when I had the opportunity. I decided to sleep on it, and keep the book a secret for now. I put it away in the bottom drawer of my chest, under a pile of sweaters. Mother never went into our drawers these days, trusting us to put away the piles of clean clothing she left on our beds, and so I knew that, for the time being at least, the grimoire would be safe there.

Placing the bridle on the headboard above my head as Lobelia had suggested, I climbed back in bed and reached up to hold the rein. Before long I slipped into a calm, dreamless sleep.

I woke to find the covers pushed back on Poppy's bed as though a sudden noise had awoken her, just as it had me.

'Poppy?' I murmured.

Feeling a little disorientated from my unusually heavy sleep I got up and went downstairs. I found the front door open again. I frowned, wondering if I had been sleepwalking the night before (something I did on occasion) and I had opened the door and left it that way.

I glanced at the grandfather clock. It was still so early that neither of my parents was awake.

'Poppy? Where are you?' I said entering the kitchen, and then searching the lounge.

She was nowhere to be seen.

I was a little frustrated because I had decided to talk to her about my dream. It was inconvenient that she was nowhere to be found.

'Probably in the outhouse,' I murmured, stifling a yawn.

Deciding this must be the case, I returned to my room. There I climbed back in bed and promptly fell back to sleep.

'Where's your sister?' Mother said, shaking me roughly by the shoulder.

I opened my eyes and turned to see Poppy's bed still empty, just as I had dreamed it had been.

'I don't know,' I said.

'Are you sure you don't know where she is?' Mother asked. Her eyes were filled with fear and my father was marching frantically back and forth in the kitchen.

'No. I thought she had gone to the outhouse,' I said.

After a thorough search of the house, grounds and stable my

father went to fetch the local constable.

'I came downstairs,' my mother said when he left, 'and I found the front door open. I thought it had been you that had gone out for fresh air, Olive. I know how restless you are sometimes, but when I realised it was Poppy, I knew something was wrong.'

'The door was open?' I asked surprised.

I knew without a shadow of doubt that I had closed it that morning, and if my nightly excursion was not a dream, I had also closed it on my return from the stable.

The constable came and questioned both my mother and me.

'You didn't hear anything?' he asked.

'No,' I said.

I didn't tell him about the dream but once he had gone, I returned to my bedroom and sat on my bed.

They say twins can sense each other. I had never experienced it because we had seldom been apart. But there was no mistaking that I felt an absence where Poppy should have been. I tested the emotion, afraid that this was all in my imagination too. Just as that insane dream, and the gypsy Lobelia must have been.

I lay back on my bed and looked up at the ceiling. There in my eye line was the bridle.

I sat up and looked around the room. If the bridle was there what of the grimoire?

I hurried to my chest of drawers and opened the bottom drawer, pushing aside the sweaters. On exposure to the light, the grimoire illuminated and greeted me as it had the night before.

This was no dream. Lobelia had been real, and so was everything she told me. But where was Poppy?

'Olive!' called Mother. 'We are going into the village to do a thorough search for Poppy. Come down and join us, I don't want to leave you home alone.'

'Yes, Mother!'

I placed the grimoire back in my drawer and covered it once more. Then I closed the drawer and headed back towards the door. I paused and looked back at Poppy's possessions, and my eyes fell on the bottle of perfume on her dresser. I was drowned with an overwhelming feeling of sadness. I had the sense that Poppy was lost to us and I couldn't shake the feeling because like it or not, I *knew* she no longer inhabited our world. *Déjà vu* rushed up to greet me with a rush of dizziness.

'When you feel this way,' Lobelia's voice whispered inside my head, 'then you know the truth already. Some outcomes can be changed, others are already determined.'

The search continued for days. The weeks passed by with no leads.

'Any news Father?' I asked when he returned from one of his meetings with the constable.

'Several people were interviewed,' he sighed sinking into his chair at the kitchen table. 'No one has seen her.'

Then months passed. Poppy's disappearance remained a mystery. It wasn't long before the local police gave up on her, and no amount of badgering from my parents could change their mind. Poppy was gone and the longer it went on, the colder the trail became.

Naturally I was devastated. I didn't dare tell anyone about the mysterious gypsy and my grimoire. I didn't think they were connected and wanted to assume, like everyone else, that somehow Poppy had gone outside. What had happened to her after that we could only speculate.

Those were awful times and my mother never really recovered from her loss. Many months later I would pass by her room at night and hear her crying. Sometimes I would find her in the kitchen staring at her recipe book. She stopped cooking Poppy's favourite dishes and Father and I never asked why because we already knew the answer.

I carried a terrible guilt inside me. I believed that somehow I was the cause of my sister's disappearance. That by taking on the grimoire I had done something evil.

I kept replaying one of the phrases, so casually given by

Lobelia: 'Sacrifices may have to be made'.

Even so, I couldn't accept that she was dead. No. There was something more to this mystery and I was determined to learn what it was. The truth would be revealed and the world would be right again.

And so, one day, I took the grimoire out of my drawer and opened it up.

As I turned the pages a whole new world opened up to me. The words lit up on each page, and despite them being written in that peculiar hieroglyphic I understood every word. So began the practicing of Lobelia's training and my real education started.

I threw myself into the study of witchcraft in the hope that I would find answers, and possibly even find my sister. But as I learned more and more of my craft, I also began to believe that Poppy had disappeared for some higher purpose. The grimoire blocked my every question relating to her and showed me new knowledge in its wake. It helped me come to terms with her absence, which was a constant ache in my heart. It eased my grief and my guilt. Although, the weight of her absence never truly left me.

I took up the duties of guardianship of Devil's End and my unusual senses grew stronger and clearer. I learnt to trust my instincts and to recognise good from bad on sight. And this talent grew stronger with every passing day.

Two years later as I walked through the village, returning from an errand, I came across another gypsy.

'Good luck charms for sale,' she said.

A sick feeling hit the pit of my stomach as the woman approached. There was not the lovely warmth I'd felt when first I met the old gypsy Lobelia who gave me the grimoire, but rather a cold, bottomless dread. This gypsy witch was far different from me and my ancestors.

She stopped a few steps away and I could feel her gaze on me. It made my skin crawl, as though I were instantly covered in small biting insects.

'You miss her,' she said. 'Your sister, Poppy.'

I stepped back, shocked by her words. 'Who told you about that?'

'I have my ways,' said the gypsy. 'What's important is, I can help you find her …'

By then the police had completely given up on Poppy. Although my parents and I always hoped to see her again. Briefly I envisaged the reunion, especially with my mother and I'll admit that the temptation to find her, and to know the truth did fill my mind and heart.

The gypsy was watching me with sharp, beady eyes as these thoughts drifted through my head. She reminded me of a bird of prey, on the lookout for carrion.

But I remembered the words of my ancestor and I slowly backed away.

'My master can give you anything you desire,' said the gypsy witch. 'All you have to do is follow Him.'

'No,' I said.

'Then you will be someone who is in His way …' said the gypsy. 'You don't want to get in the way of my master …'

I was only 19 and still so unsure of my power as a witch. The grimoire had warned of temptations that would come my way. This one was preying on my darkest need to bring my sister home and relieve the suffering of my parents.

I'm not ashamed to admit that the gypsy scared me. Her eyes held me for a moment before I turned and ran. It was the final straw to push my fear and urge for self preservation over the edge. I did so because I saw her eyes change and the blackness of Hell was reflected in her gaze.

I returned home. I ran upstairs and pulled the grimoire from its hiding place, holding it closely to my chest as I recalled Lobelia's parting words.

Was it just two short years ago when she gave me this book? I wondered.

'Beware of the temptations, Olive,' she had told me. 'They'll offer you anything to turn you from good to evil. Just remember that whatever the reward, the price you'll pay will never be worth it. Keep true to your beliefs and I promise that all will be well.'

And, although I found it somewhat hard to believe that all would be well in this case, I knew that I would never give in to the darkness of black magic.

From that day onwards, the grimoire revealed more magic to me than it ever had. I opened it and it showed me a ward against evil.

I prepared and purified my altar, which was now always on top of Poppy's old dresser. My parents never came in the room anymore and I took sole responsibility for cleaning it. Therefore I knew my altar would never be disturbed.

I lit two white candles and chanted the spell. Then I visualized a blue light, first surrounding me, and then our home. After that I spread the veil of protection over the entire village, cleansing it of the gypsy witch's malignance.

I did not realize it but that was the moment when I truly took on the role of guardian.

My apprenticeship had ended.

HALF LIGHT
Suzanne Barbieri

1

This light – a light unlike any other – casts crescent-shaped shadows. They are scattered all around, like confetti moons. The village children laugh and dance on the green opposite The Cloven Hoof, the younger ones try to catch the shapes in their hands.

'I nearly had one, but it got away,' a little girl tells her mother. 'I wanted to put it in a jar to make a spell.'

I allow myself a smile. I shall keep an eye on that one.

'It's coming!' someone shouts as the sky darkens.

'Don't look at it!' cries another.

Some of us turn our backs and gaze down into our rudimentary, home-made pinhole projectors; others look up, their eyes shielded with protective glasses.

'Oh, it's beautiful. The Diamond Ring!'

The Diamond Ring. The last bead of the Sun before the darkness.

Such is the strange alchemy of the solar eclipse. Like a wedding in reverse: first confetti moons, then the rings, and finally the darkness: empty like a life before love.

There is much magic to be had today, but it's a bitter-sweet occasion for me. I leave the revellers and head off home.

'Mind how you go, Miss Hawthorne,' a young man calls after me.

For a moment, I think I've travelled back in time, and then I realise it's young Eddie, grandson of Ned who was the barman at The Cloven Hoof until his retirement. They look so alike. Same sandy hair and red beard. Funny how fashions come and go. All the young men are wearing beards again, waistcoats too. I wouldn't be surprised if Eddie has raided Ned's wardrobe, by the look of him.

'Thank you, Eddie. Is your grandfather coming out today?'

'He's not up to it, to be honest, but I'll tell him you said hello. Though I'm sure he'd still like a visit when you've got a minute. Maybe you could drop in for a cup of tea some afternoon; chat about old times, and all that. It'd do him the world of good.'

'Yes, I shall. That's very thoughtful of you. What a blessing to have such a considerate grandson.'

Eddie seems embarrassed by the compliment. Just like his grandfather would have been.

'I'm meant to be getting the upstairs rooms ready before my bar shift starts, but the guests won't be arriving until this evening, so I can walk you home if you like,' Eddie says.

'There's no need, really. Tell you what: why don't I drop in on your grandfather now? It's on my way, and I could do with the company myself.'

The eclipse alone brings back no end of memories, but in mistaking young Eddie for Ned, something deeply buried has stirred. Truth be told, I need to talk to Ned about the old days, but I don't know how much he remembers. We've all noticed how forgetful he's become. Perhaps it's old age, perhaps something worse. But no matter. I'll take tea with Ned, if only to relieve his grandson of the burden of care for a while.

I arrive at Ned's cottage to find him standing on the doorstep. He is agitated, and I resist the temptation to label this a symptom at least until we have spoken.

'There you are, Miss Olive! I thought you'd forgotten,' he says, and I realise that I had forgotten.

It was a ritual we observed for quite a while when we were younger, a ritual we let slide as time went on and memories faded. In the years that followed … the event, Ned and I would meet after an eclipse to discuss our thoughts and memories of those earlier days. As time passed, it all became less clear, or rather we spun explanations that enabled us to file it away in the deeper recesses of our minds.

'Come in then,' Ned says. 'I'll put the kettle on.'

I can't tell whether Ned's expectation of my visit is a sign that his memory is still sharp and he has new ideas to discuss, or if it means that he has forgotten we abandoned our post-eclipse meetings and is living in some half-constructed past of a confused mind.

'In the garden,' Ned calls out, as I make my way through his rooms. 'We'll catch the last of the eclipse. Things look different in the half light.'

He's right. The garden is filled with strange shadows. It's as though we've passed through a portal into another world that is both comforting yet oddly disconcerting.

Ned sets the tea tray on the wrought-iron table and sits opposite me.

'Iron keeps the faery folk away,' he pats the table and winks. 'Not that I've anything against them, but I'm too old to deal with their mischief.'

'Some of us get no respite, even in our dotage.'

'Your dotage is a long way off, Miss Olive. Mine, on the other hand …' He leans towards me and continues in a conspiratorial tone. 'They think I've lost my marbles, you know.'

'Who'd be so cruel as to say that, Ned?'

'No one's said anything, but I know what they're thinking. The thing is … I'm afraid they might be right.'

'What do you mean?'

'I get confused. Not all the time. But now and again, I think I'm somewhere else … no that's not right. Not somewhere; some *when*.'

A shiver runs the length of my spine. The exact same feeling I had when I saw young Eddie. Mistaking him for Ned was only part of it. There was a time slip, of that I'm certain. Before I can voice this to Ned, he continues.

'When I was waiting for you just now … I knew you'd be coming, even though we haven't met up on such an occasion for years. It was as though the past and the present came together …'

he stops and shakes his head. 'No wonder the villagers think I'm off my rocker. I don't blame them.'

'I felt it too,' I say quietly. 'I ran into your grandson earlier. I thought he was you. Not just because of the resemblance. It felt just as it had back then.'

'You know what that means, don't you, Miss Olive?' Ned says.

'I'm not entirely sure that I do.'

'When the past makes itself felt in the present, there's unfinished business.'

I watch the shadows move across Ned's garden, and take a moment to compose myself before I acknowledge what I know to be true.

'I fear you may be right,' I say with an ill-concealed sigh. 'I have noticed a sense of … not exactly change, more something reaching its completion. Loose ends need to be tied.'

'You still have it, don't you?'

'The silver box you made for me? My treasure chest. Of course. Safely sealed.'

'For now at least,' Ned says.

'I wouldn't!' I protest.

'Not you, but neither of us will be here to guard it forever. I might have to sound out young Eddie.'

'You really think …?'

'No, but if I'm going to be cast as a lunatic, I'm taking you with me!' Ned lets out an uproarious laugh. For a moment he is his old self again.

By the time I leave Ned, the eclipse is long gone, and the Sun is high in a clear blue sky.

I cannot count the times I've taken this path from The Cloven Hoof to my cottage, with the occasional stop by Ned's house. It is a journey usually so uneventful, that every step is instantly forgotten. Apart from that one night … And here we are, home already. Journey forgotten as soon as made.

Today is a day of shadows and half light. Even the Sun wore

a cloak for a while, so I'll close the curtains and light candles, and that will be illumination enough to look back upon these memories. I shall rest my bones in this old chair and follow my mind wherever it takes me. I have my crystal ball, my treasure chest, and a good red wine, so forgive me if I become maudlin.

This box I call my treasure chest. Solid silver, beautifully engraved. Ned knew, of course, today of all days, the desire to open it is strong. But I won't. I've sealed it with wax and charms to ensure my foolish heart doesn't overrule my stubborn head.

'Love looks not with the eyes, but with the mind.' According to the Bard's Helena.

And it is true. Sometimes. Ned was right. Things are different in the half light: beautiful, magical … alive. And people become different. They dare to dream of lives unlived, paths less travelled.

As I look down at my crystal, I catch sight of a face I haven't seen in decades. A young woman looks back at me. I am not surprised. In fact, I've been expecting her. Today the past and the present meet each other head on. The young woman is me. And I have unfinished business. I have fought this for too long. It is time to go back and face it …

2

I cannot stop thinking about that man.

I don't know what it all means yet, but this is the third time he's appeared in my crystal. He was barely an outline at first; then a hazy silhouette. Now he has a distinct shape, but still no face. I should wait to see how things play out, but this has been a funny few months for me.

I suppose it began around my birthday, which is always a time of mixed feelings, remembering Poppy …

And I'd heard people talking, *poor Olive, all alone*.

I'd assumed they meant the loss of my twin, but then I heard the word *spinster*, said in that pitying tone. That was how they saw me. An old maid, all alone with only her cat for company.

Not that I care what they think, but I'd only just turned thirty!

It was around that time that he first appeared. Perhaps I conjured him up, a dream man to whisk me away and silence the gossips. But I don't think so. A witch I may be; fanciful I am not.

And yet here he is.

Ah! A glimpse of his face, then he turns away. I can feel him gently mocking me, as if … as if he knows I'm watching him. What does this mean?

I reach into the pouch and pull out three runes.

Thurisaz: a thorn that stabs at the heart, temptation, a warning.

Hm, now that is interesting. Perhaps the tall, dark stranger is my knight errant after all.

Ansuz: communication, the power of words, revelation.

Could he be a teacher? A rival? Will I have a magickal battle on my hands. Calm down, Olive. Always over-thinking.

Dagaz: daylight, breakthrough, a new dawn.

All's well that ends well, then. But how exciting! It will be good to have some new blood in the village, even if he's only passing through.

I glance at the crystal again. He's still there. He *does* know I'm seeing him. Can he see me too? He's calling to me. We have a bond. That thought surprises me. But I feel it so strongly.

I need to clear my head. It's a warm night, too warm to stay inside. I decide to go for a walk, maybe drop by The Cloven Hoof for a dose of Ned's common sense.

From the open doorway of The Cloven Hoof, the sweetest sound drifts towards me. Long, melancholy notes forming perhaps the saddest tune I have ever heard. I want to weep, laugh, dance; almost as if I am under a spell.

I step over the threshold and follow the music. The pub is crowded and I have to push my way through to get to the bar. The haunting melody of a solo violin cuts through the burble of conversation and I turn towards it.

'Good evening, Miss Olive,' Ned says. 'What's your poison?'

I can't take in what Ned's saying, because I've found the

source of the music, and nothing else in the world exists.

A man … *the* man, the one in my crystal, sits in the corner, a violin under his chin. His clothes and hair are black, and his skin pale. A man made of moonlight, dressed in the night sky.

Some might think it strange to call a man beautiful, but he is. His hair is long, like his fingers, like the notes he plays on his violin, like his gaze that burns into me, and pulls at me as though he is a magnet and I have iron filings dancing in my stomach.

'Miss Olive …?' Ned repeats.

And the spell is broken.

A drink … I should want something cold on such a warm night, but in my mind an image forms of an ornate chalice filled with dark wine. This is an unusual craving. I want it so, that wine, but I cannot speak to ask for it.

A voice at my side speaks for me, 'The lady will have a glass of red wine.'

A shiver runs through me. Not just because the stranger seems to have read my thoughts; the air around me has turned quite cold.

'My name is Victor,' he says, his voice soft, cultured, melodic.

I avoid his gaze, embarrassed that he might see in my face what his beauty has stirred in me.

'Olive,' I reply, failing to disguise the tremor in my voice. 'Olive Hawthorne.'

I steel myself, then turn my face to meet his.

Oh, those eyes.

My breath catches in my throat. He smiles softly and holds my gaze with his deep, grey eyes. I have never seen such eyes. A storm cloud; granite; a shade which might be the exact mid-point between coal and a diamond. A wolf's eyes.

My heart is pierced with the blind god's arrow. *Thurisaz.*

I don't know how I got home last night, unless I was carried on soft, black wings.

I awake feeling different in a way I can't explain. *Portentous.* That's the word that comes to mind. Something of momentous significance is on the horizon, and I must go to meet it.

I decide to have my lunch at The Cloven Hoof in the hope of seeing Victor again. I have to know …

'Afternoon, Miss Olive,' Ned says. Then, with a wink, 'Glass of red?'

'Just a menu please, Ned,' I try not to rise to the bait, but curiosity overrides embarrassment, and I have to ask. 'The gentleman who bought my drink last night … is he around? I think it only fair I return the favour.'

'As it happens, he's staying in one of the upstairs rooms, but you're too early. Sleeps all day and never rises before evening. So you'll have to come back then. Menu's on the board.'

'Thank you,' I reply and make a show of pondering the specials.

'Menu's always on the board, as well you know. Anyone'd think you have something on your mind.' Ned barely disguises a smirk.

'I'll keep my mind on my business, and you keep your mind on yours.'

'Charmed, I'm sure. Here …' Ned leans towards me, 'Do you reckon he's one of those Beatnik types?'

He means it as a light-hearted slur, but I can only see the glamour in the term: Beat Generation poets in their black garb; modern philosophers raging against an unfeeling world.

'Ah, the Blessed Ones,' I say.

'Eh?'

'Jack Kerouac associated the word "Beat" with "Beatitude". He felt this generation to be blessed.'

'Can't argue with that,' Ned says. 'I'd feel pretty blessed if I got to lie in bed all day.'

I don't care what Ned thinks. I don't care what any of them think. I have made up my mind to see Victor this evening.

I walk on air to The Cloven Hoof as the Sun sinks behind me like a gold doubloon thrown into a deep red sea. *Red sky at night, witch's delight.* A blush rises on my cheeks and I smile to myself. I can feel Victor calling to me. This is no spinster's imagination: this is what we both want.

When I walk into The Cloven Hoof heads turn, as if I've made a deliberate entrance. *En-trance* ... I entrance them, as Victor has entranced me. They can see we are different. Powerful. And I wonder again if he is a warlock, come to share his wisdom with me.

I see him. Seated in a corner, his violin on the floor resting against his chair. He beckons me, and I take the seat next to him.

How is it morning? Hasn't the Sun just set? Am I not with Victor, discussing the world and its wonders? The first rays of the morning Sun force their way through the gaps in my curtains, but it can't be. Who stole the night?

I was with Victor, in The Cloven Hoof. I know I was. Yet here it is strange: I don't remember anything we talked about, except that we seemed to cover every subject under the Sun, and it felt as if we were thinking each other's thoughts. I know I didn't dream that.

But there *was* a dream ...

A dream so vivid it still plays when I close my eyes.

We were in an old house; grand, a mansion. And there were two of him. Two Victors. One at my side, the calm, elegant man I knew; and another ... Oh, the thought of him makes me shudder: a raging, wild creature beating his fists against glass. The glass is a mirror. Yes, I see it now. This frantic being, this other Victor, is trapped behind the glass of a mirror. For a moment, it almost made sense, then ...

I woke. Or at least I thought I did. Heart racing, I jolted out of the first dream into another, and the sound of a baby crying. That truly woke me. I sat up and glanced around my room, half expecting to see a crib. I know it was a dream, but it felt so real. And I knew the child in the crib was not just any child, but my own. Could it ...

So many thoughts … I've always assumed I'll marry some day, that I will have an heir onto whom I can pass my knowledge. Someone to take over the guardianship of Devil's End. Lately, I've felt that time is running out. Am I swayed by village gossip, or do I really feel like that?

Is this what the runes meant? Is Victor to be …? I hardly dare let myself think it. Why should this man look at me that way when he must have women falling at his feet? And yet …

We arranged to meet again tonight, that I do remember. Would it be too much to wear my best dress? No, it's too soon. He can take me as I am, or not at all. But it's only morning and I have hours to kill. What shall I do with myself?

No. Stop. This is so unlike me. These thoughts are not mine. How can I be so enamoured of someone I hardly know? I must force all thoughts of him from my mind, at least for the moment: I have herbs to gather.

This time I won't forget.

I am wearing a charm to help me remember: a tiny cloth bag, filled with herbs and dried flowers, sewn inside my slip. I call it my Ophelia Charm.

'There's rosemary, that's for remembrance …' as Ophelia said. Not only memory. It can protect against evil spirits, and keep bad dreams at bay. 'And there is pansies, that's for thoughts,'

And more besides. Fennel, Columbine, Daisy, Rue … plus some additions of my own. But of course, yet again I take inspiration from Shakespeare. A kind of Bibliomancy, of sorts. My own invention, I like to think. Although it has likely been done before: poetry for spells; stories as rituals; the words of a play used as incantations. The Bard has never failed me yet. Give me strength, sweet William.

Back in The Cloven Hoof, Victor escorts me up to his room. Eyes turn towards us. Is the spinster still a maid? Let them wonder.

The curtains are closed and the room is lit by candles. A

romantic gesture, dare I hope?

How very odd. Victor has covered the mirrors. And it's not as though he lacks vanity. When I entered the pub, I caught him preening; touching his hair, running his fingers over the contours of his face. And on the wall opposite the bed, he has hung a painted portrait of himself at which he glances often.

This reminds me of the mirror in my dream. Is Victor attempting to conquer his vanity? An admirable pursuit, if so; but why shouldn't the beautiful gaze upon themselves occasionally? Why should they curse their looks because of others' envy? Not that I have to worry about that …

'But you are beautiful, Olive,' Victor says. 'Let no one say otherwise.'

I am caught off-guard. Did I speak aloud, or has he read my thoughts?

'You think I haven't heard how the villagers talk about us?' he continues. So there is an 'us'. 'They think I am using you, beguiling you in some way.'

'Well, such a handsome man spending time with a plain woman …'

'Olive, you are far from plain. Anyone who calls you so is blind, shallow, and envious.'

'That's very kind …'

'I am not kind. I say only what is true. You have a light unlike any other. It dances in your eyes like a forest fire. You're a nature spirit. Look at your hair: tangled briars tamed with a pin. Your mouth is a rose without thorns. And your sweet, wise words are the nectar in its heart.'

'Goodness me!' My thoughts race, and I cannot make sense of the situation.

'I have embarrassed you. I apologise. But let me tell you what I most desire in you. It is your wonderful mind. Your thoughts buzz about your head like bees around their queen. I feel as if I could catch them out of the air.'

He makes a snatching motion above my head. My mind becomes quiet and I am calm.

'Please sit,' he says. And I obey. 'Now, listen: "The difficulty,

43

my friends, is not in avoiding death …" Who am I quoting?'

The answer is on the tip of my tongue, so near and yet so far.

'"But in avoiding unrighteousness …",' he continues, and I have the answer.

'"For that runs faster than death." Plato. The Apology of Socrates.' I answer triumphantly.

'Very good. I have a translation here. Would you read to me?'

Victor hands me the book. It is old and looks valuable, perhaps priceless. I open it carefully, and touch the pages as lightly as if they were moth's wings.

'And afterwards,' Victor says. 'We can discuss which gods we serve.'

Yet again, an untimely dawn has swept the night away, and I am alone in my room. It must have been a warm night, for I have kicked my bed covers off. Either that, or my sleep was fitful. Though if I dreamed, I do not recall it.

I remember more this time, but not everything. I sense a darkness in Victor, but one not of his own making. Whatever it is, he is not ready to share it with me, even though we have shared so much, or at least, I think we have, I cannot be sure. Victor controls the conversation and my memory of it.

Think, girl, think!

We talked … about the idea of different gods. Yes. Inspired by Socrates' belief in the guiding spirits, the voices in his head, his *Daimons*. Lesser gods, but not demons … this was important … something about dark spirits, other entities … Oh, why can't I remember? It was a warning … Yes! A coming darkness for which we both had to prepare.

And prepare I have. Tonight I will cook a special meal for us. I feel I know Victor well enough to invite him into my home. Even though we've spent hours alone in his room, he has always been the perfect gentleman, and has never done more than kiss my hand. I shall show him my treasures: my crystal, my runes.

Perhaps he will allow me to divine what lies in his future. Yes. This is good. I am convinced that if we meet on my own territory, I will not forget our conversation.

'No!' Victor says, far too emphatically. 'You must never invite me into your home. Promise me you will never do that.'

Whatever have I done to make him so angry? He reads my bitter disappointment, my unease at his harsh tone, and he softens.

'Dear Olive, I didn't mean to frighten you. And please know that I am not rejecting you or your friendship. I wish I could tell you, right now, the reason I cannot visit you, but in time you will understand.'

I take a few deep breaths and feel myself begin to calm down.

'And I apologise most humbly for my brutish tone. I am not in good spirits today,' he says.

How selfish of me. Now that I look at him, I can see in his face that he is feeling unwell. His skin is even paler than usual, and there are dark shadows beneath his eyes.

'No, it is I who should apologise. I can see you are tired, and I've been taking up far too much of your time with my idle chatter.'

'Not you, Olive. I live for our discussions. You have brought me a joy I thought I'd never see again. Come tomorrow. Usual time. I promise I will be in finer fettle.'

It would be a shame to waste the extra food I'd prepared, so I decided to take it to Ned on my way to meet Victor. Ned's not working tonight, and left to his own devices at home, he won't eat properly.

Only he doesn't appear to be in. Ah, I expect he's gone calling on young Sally in the next village. Lovely girl, but according to Ned, she's no better cook than he is. Well, there's enough here for two if Sally decides to come back with him. I'll just leave the dish on the doorstep.

I'd expected to be able to kill a little time chatting to Ned, so it's too early to meet Victor. I'll have to take the scenic route through the graveyard.

Some people are afraid of cemeteries, but I find them peaceful. Especially now, with the Sun newly set and the scent of freshly laid flowers in the air. I watch the sky change from red to violet, and immerse myself in the lingering earthbound spirits. I feel at home among the dead. They have stories to tell. Sometimes I can hear their voices whisper to me faintly, like a breeze through the trees.

But wait … what's that? An altogether different sound. The scrabbling of hooves, panicked breaths; the cry of a desperate animal, then a sound like a beast biting into flesh.

I should run, but instead of turning to flee, my feet carry me towards the affray. I am less afraid than I should be. Why is that? This is more than simple curiosity. Some strange force is keeping me here, pushing me forward. I feel as if I am outside myself. I am both a part of this and an observer. I don't want to look, yet I am compelled. There is a creeping sense of inevitability. This is something I already know, but must witness in order to acknowledge. The rest of the world falls away as I focus on what is ahead of me.

There, by a grave overgrown with weeds, caught in the purple glow of the almost-night sky, is Victor, his teeth buried in the neck of a still-twitching deer.

He looks up and sees me. His eyes are wide and fierce, and his mouth dark with the animal's blood. Victor's hold over me dissipates. I turn and run, but he is hot on my heels.

'Olive, please,' he calls after me. 'You are in no danger. I would never harm you.'

But still I run. Through the graveyard, through the village, I run from this creature at my back. Other Victor. The wild man in the mirror. My feet sting and my hair shakes itself loose from its bun.

I run until I reach my cottage. It is only when I stop, heart pounding and feet stinging, that I realise: he could have caught me at any moment, but he chose not to. I am safe with him.

I press my back against the door of my cottage. Victor stands facing me, a short distance away. I look up at him, and am about to speak, but he stops me.

'Do not invite me in,' he says. 'Come, we'll go to The Cloven Hoof.'

I know what people are thinking when we arrive breathless and flustered; Victor dishevelled, me with my hair loose about my shoulders. Everyone stops talking. We walk to the stairs in silence, but I feel the weight of their judgement burning into our backs. The moment we are out of eyeshot, their chatter commences, but I don't care about groundless gossip. I've endured worse. Not everybody trusts a witch. So Victor and I have something else in common.

I follow Victor up the stairs to his room. He enters ahead of me. This is no lack of manners, I understand. Had I entered first, I would, in effect, have been inviting him in.

Now I know why the mirrors are covered, and it makes me unbearably sad. That this kind, beautiful man has no reflection is a tragedy. He will never see what I see: his goodness, his intelligence, his ... *aliveness* when fired-up with ideas. He is doomed to doubt his own existence. Something normally taken for granted is forever denied him.

'I am deeply sorry you had to see that,' he says. 'This is why I ask you to come late, so that I have time to ... so that I have time before you arrive. It is the only way I can guarantee your safety.'

'I understand. Truly I do. And I thank you for it.'

'I want to show you something,' he says.

Victor hands me a small painting of a beautiful woman with silver-blonde hair and ghost-white skin. The woman has a strange effect on me. I feel drawn to her, fascinated in a way I can't explain; yet at the same time, something is amiss. I have divined whether people are alive or dead from a photograph before, but never have I felt such conflicting senses from a painting.

'Is this … your wife?' I ask him, barely able to form the words.

'No. This is the monster that took my wife and child from me. This is my maker. I carry her picture with me always so I will never forget what she did, and so that I will never become like her.'

My heart aches for his devastating personal tragedy. I want to ask about his family, but I dare not.

'You do not need to ask,' Victor says. 'I will tell you. I have told you. Every time we met. But this time, I promise you will remember.'

He pours me a glass of red wine. As I sip, I see the blood of the deer from which Victor fed, but even that doesn't change my belief that he is a good man.

'The pain is still raw,' he says. 'Even after a century and a half. Look at the wine, Olive. See how the surface is like a dark scrying glass.'

As I concentrate on the shining darkness, shapes begin to form.

'Very good. Now you are ready to come with me,' Victor's voice becomes distant. 'Come with me, Olive.'

'Where are we going?'

'To somewhere long ago …'

I am aware of Victor saying something more, but his words are drowned out by other sounds. I feel myself carried off and I think again of wings. I can hear the air beneath them as they beat.

We are soaring through a darkness that is very like a sky, but I know it is not. We are moving not through space, but through time. I am exhilarated. And then …

Oh, but he promised I wouldn't forget! I'm back on the green outside The Cloven Hoof, on a sunny afternoon, wracked with disappointment that once again I cannot remember Victor's story.

I am about to head home when something catches my eye. The pub sign. Whilst the name remains the same, the painting is different. The style is from a previous century, yet it looks quite new. And the people milling about the village green are also dressed in clothes of that era.

I feel suddenly disorientated. Once again, I am both actor and observer. Gradually, my unease dissipates, and I take in the marvellous spectacle. Never before have I witnessed a vision so real. Victor, you are truly a Magus!

'Look, Olive,' a voice at my side whispers. 'There I am …'

Victor takes my arm, and points towards a young couple sitting on the grass while their child plays nearby. The man in the vision is Victor, and he is a living human being. He is radiant with health, and glowing with love for his family.

'Little Abigail, and my dear Amelia. We were childhood sweethearts. Nothing could part us until …'

The scene folds back like the turned page of a book.

Night has fallen. A carriage pulls up outside The Cloven Hoof. A woman steps out, and my breath catches in my throat. It is her. Victor's maker. I know what she is, yet I am drawn to her. Her beauty surpasses her portrait, and I find myself longing to see her ethereal face close up.

'Be careful, Olive,' Victor says. 'Do not let her work her evil charms on you. None are safe from her; even in visions.'

A vision of the past affecting the future? Yet again, I have the strange feeling that time works differently here in Devil's End.

I watch, spellbound, as she glides into The Cloven Hoof, followed by Victor, who is carrying her suitcases. Of course, he was the Inn Keeper. I should have known. Past and present forever intertwined.

'Her name,' Victor continues, 'or at least the name she gave, was Lilyana. She claimed to be a visiting dignitary from some kingdom in Eastern Europe that I had never heard of. And we were all supposed to be at her beck and call.' His voice has a tone of distaste.

'You didn't like her?'

'Something was ... off about her. She was polite, charming. Everyone fell under her spell.'

'Except you.'

He hesitates, as if considering his reaction to Lilyana for the first time. Then I see what looks like realisation on his face, or perhaps the decision to finally share something he had kept to himself for too long.

'It was the way she looked at my wife and daughter. At first glance, her attitude could have been mistaken for a noblewoman's gaze upon commoners, but that wasn't it, because she didn't look at me that way at all. And, if truth be told, many thought my wife Amelia had married beneath herself in choosing me.'

'But you're the perfect gentleman.'

'You're kind, Olive, and I have had many years to learn how to present myself; but back then, the minutiae of the class system was even more pronounced, so if a high ranking person were to look down on any member of my family it would have been me. No, this was something altogether different.'

'Lilyana was in love with you, perhaps?'

'Love?' Victor says, and breathes out sharply, a single exhalation of derision. 'That creature knew nothing of love. Possession, control, hunger, all that and more, but never love.'

The scene changes again.

Victor bursts through the door of Lilyana's room in The Cloven Hoof, the same room he's staying in now. Oh, this twisted tale! I fear it will weave its way far into the future.

Lilyana is kneeling on the bed where Victor's dead wife lies, pale and still, her throat opened by a deep wound.

Lilyana's exquisite features twist into a mask of cruel satisfaction. Victor's mouth opens in a cry of despair. And then I see what lies on Amelia's breast. Oh no. This is too much to bear. The child, little Abigail, is also dead with her throat torn out.

Lilyana rises. She does not stand, but floats above the bed, her hand outstretched and beckoning, to draw Victor to her.

'I could have saved myself,' Victor whispers to me. 'I could have run, but I was a fool who believed she would understand mercy.'

The Victor of the past moves towards her, and pulls his collar away from his neck.

'I asked her to take me too, so that my family and I would all be dead together. Either she misunderstood, or she was even more cruel than I thought, for she made me like her.'

'Not like her,' I say. 'One of her kind, maybe, but not like her.'

'I am sorry to burden you with this, Olive.'

'It's no burden. It is the part of the honour of friendship. The rough with the smooth, the sour with the sweet …'

'The living with the dead,' he says, and then I notice the vision has gone and we are back in the present time in the room where all this happened.

'The grave where you saw me feed. It is their grave. Abigail and Amelia. United in death in a way I can never be a part of.'

The power of his revelation, his openness, humbles me. *Ansuz*.

Victor bows his head, the weight of his sorrow all but crushes him. I rest my hand on his clenched fist. He looks up at me.

'See? I cannot even cry. I am a shadow of a man. Numb. Inhuman.'

'No,' I say, but there is no comforting him.

He shakes his head. 'I am nothing,' he says.

'You are a good man, who lived and loved. No one can take that from you.'

'But they did. And it was those very traits that were my undoing. She said it was my passion she craved. My single-minded devotion to my family made my essence more desirable. She decided to make a companion of me, to make me like her: Undead, never to walk in the Sun or be free to love again. Many would have accepted their fate and followed her to the ends of the Earth. I refused. I would rather be alone for eternity than spend a second in her company.'

'It doesn't have to be that way,' I say, barely able to look him in the eyes.

Victor touches my chin and gently turns my face up towards his.

'Dear Olive, if only that were possible. You remind me of my wife in many ways. You are a pure, honest woman with so much love to give. I wish I could be the one to share your life, but you deserve so much more that I could ever give you.'

That's when the thought comes to me. Perhaps I'm not thinking clearly. Perhaps I am still bewitched by the vision, but at this moment, it seems to be the only thing that makes sense. What if the village gossips are correct? What if I am destined to be an old maid? Without a husband, there will be no heir onto whom to pass my knowledge. But what if that didn't matter? I wouldn't need an heir if I could live forever …

'Perhaps there is a way.' I turn my head and bare my throat.

An image forms in my mind of that ancient sculpture of a woman, head thrown back in ecstasy as an angel fills her with divine love. It is less a mental image and more a projection behind my closed eyelids. It has to be a sign, that image of Bridal Mysticism, the marriage of a human soul and a divine being. Perhaps Victor will find peace in our Chymical Wedding and in having a companion for eternity.

Instead, he is furious.

'No, no, no! This is exactly what I feared.'

Victor grasps my shoulders and I snap out of my delusion.

'This is not you,' he says softly. 'This is her. I told you she can reach you even through a vision. Time, reality, life, death; they are all toys to her. Everything is but a game.'

'But really, is it such a bad idea? We could share the guardianship of Devil's End. We would be strong, invincible …'

'We would be monsters. How could we protect the village when we would represent its greatest threat?'

'What threat would we be? You take the blood of animals, I saw you.'

'Sometimes,' he says. 'That isn't possible.'

I know he is telling me that he has killed and will kill again. I shudder. Even though I know it's true, I don't want to believe it.

'My deepest regret is that you and I never got to walk together in daylight,' Victor says. 'But I know something that you and your villagers have missed.'

I look at him quizzically. He smiles, and I am comforted.

'Tomorrow, at noon,' he continues. 'There will be a total eclipse.'

'But that's not for another month. My charts …'

'Your charts are wrong, Olive. I will come to your cottage a little before noon tomorrow. Be waiting outside for me.'

The Sun is high in the sky. It beats down onto me, a constant drone behind the rhythm of my pounding heart. I feel like … yes, I'll say it: I feel like a bride who has arrived ahead of the groom.

In this moment, I am at a crossroads. If Victor doesn't come, I'll go back to my life as the village spinster, young in years, but old in spirit. Too old to be a maiden, never a mother, not yet a crone. If he does, I stand on the threshold of a thousand possibilities. Will I go away with him, discover new lands, learn new magic; or will we stay here to safeguard the village for eternity?

Finally, I have my answer. The same blacked-out carriage that brought Lilyana to the village pulls up in the road by my cottage. As Victor steps out, I hold my breath in anticipation. He is dressed from head to toe in black, his face covered with a black veil.

'It is nearly time, my dear Olive,' he says as he walks along the path towards me. He takes my hand, kisses it through the veil, then steps back. 'Nearly time …'

I glance up at the sky. The Sun still burns fiercely.

'Victor …?' I say.

'I do this for you, Olive. It is the only way.'

He pulls off his veil, then his cloak and his black leather gloves, and casts them aside.

'Victor! No! It's too soon!'

The moment the sunlight touches him, his skin ignites. He cries out in agony as his flesh disintegrates.

I grab his cloak up off the ground and rush to cover him with it, but as it touches his smouldering form, it too catches light. I try to beat out the glowing embers, but he turns to dust beneath my hands. With his ashes still on my skin, I feel his spirit pass through me in joyous ecstasy to be free at last.

And I realise. This had been his plan all along. The eclipse is not until next month, my charts are correct. This was the only way he could protect me from himself. I could have stopped him. If I'd paid attention instead of filling my head with silly fantasies, I'd have noticed the shapes of the shadows were wrong and known there wasn't to be an eclipse, just a blazing hot summer's day. *Dagaz.*

Without thinking, I make to brush Victor's ashes from my hands onto my skirt. Before I can do so, someone grasps my wrists and hauls me to my feet. A familiar face blocks the Sun. I squint up at him.

'Ned? What are you doing here?'

'I saw, Miss Olive. I saw …'

'Oh, Ned, I … I'm so sorry … He did it out of kindness, to protect us …'

Tears come then, for so many things: for Victor and his family, for their lives cut short, for his life: ended yet never-ending; and for myself, mourning the loss of possibilities.

'Not this,' Ned continues. 'I saw before. In the graveyard.'

'The graveyard …?'

'The night you left supper for me on my doorstep. I'd gone to see Sally, but she had her Great Aunt staying, and they didn't want me hanging around. I must have missed you by two minutes, so I came after you to say thank you. That's when I saw him. And I'm ashamed to say, I ran.'

'So did I, Ned. But if he'd wanted to catch either of us, he would have easily done so.'

'I realised that after I pulled myself together, so I decided to keep an eye on him. And to make preparations.'

'Preparations?'

Ned takes the bag he has slung over his shoulder and places it on the ground. From inside he retrieves an ornately carved silver box.

'This is probably all we need now,' he says.

'Why? What else did you bring?' I ask.

Ned looks at me wryly. I know the answer of course: holy water, crucifix, stake, garlic.

'Oh, and this,' he brandishes a hearth set consisting of a small brush and shovel. 'Probably best if you do this, Miss Olive,' Ned hands me the hearth set, 'It's what he would have wanted.'

I am deeply touched by Ned's honouring of Victor's needs. He could have seen him as a monster, but has chosen to share my trust in Victor. Ned is a true friend. In joy and in pain.

After sweeping up Victor's ashes, I pick up the box and hug it to my chest, unsure of what to do. After a moment, Ned takes the box from me and leads me back inside my cottage.

'Now seal it with wax,' he says.

He places the silver box full of ashes on my table, and we sit down opposite each other. I pick up a short, wide candle. The centre of it has worn down enough that there is ample wax pooling around its wick.

'And say something.' Ned says.

'What?'

'Say some kind of spell. Sealing, protecting, you know the kind of thing.'

3

The scene in my crystal becomes hazy then disappears and is replaced by my reflection. I am no longer a young woman, but the memories are sharper than ever. Hard to believe that was fifty years ago … oh, good heavens! Fifty years exactly.

Now I know why Ned was waiting for me. He must have

known unconsciously, but couldn't make sense of his intuition. The past making itself felt in the present. Unfinished business, indeed.

I make my way back to Ned's house as fast as I can, but my body doesn't want to comply. I feel as if I'm pushing against a tremendous force. Is this just frustration that my speed cannot match my eagerness, or is there something more?

A wind blows up, and with it, dusk falls. This is not right. It is barely late afternoon, and this is not the season for gales. Oh dear. Hold on, Ned. I hope I am in time.

Finally, I reach Ned's cottage. The sky is black. Midnight has come hours early. I hammer repeatedly on the door.

'Hold your horses,' Ned calls from inside. 'Where's the fire?'

He opens the door, and looks confused when he sees me.

'Olive?' he says. 'Whatever's happened?'

I must look a sight. I am quite out of breath and the wind has played havoc my hair.

'Weren't you just here …?'

'A couple of hours ago, yes,'

'And why's it so dark? Have I been asleep?' he says, his confusion all too apparent.

I usher Ned inside, then bolt the door behind us.

'This reminds me of something …' he says.

'Oh … of course. Sit down, and I'll explain.'

I realise what he means. He's remembering the night I turned up breathless and dishevelled at The Cloven Hoof. The night we ran from Victor. The night we learned the truth.

'I don't like this one bit,' Ned shakes his head as he paces the room. 'I knew I was right. I've been saying it over and over, but not a soul believed me. They think I'm mad, you know. They want to put me away.'

'No one will put you anywhere. Not while I've breath in my body. Sit down, Ned. We have a lot to talk about.'

Ned switches on the tall lamp by his rocking chair and plumps the cushions before easing himself into the seat.

'I knew this time was important. It's two hundred years, you see,' he says.

'Yes, I know.'

'Two hundred years since your man was ... made. They do come back, you know.'

'The box is still sealed, I promise you.'

'Not him,' Ned whispers. 'His maker.'

She who can reach through visions. She for whom time means nothing. She who is the bane of Devil's End. Did I summon her by reliving the vision?

'Oh dear,' I say. 'I fear this may be my fault.'

'Don't you say that, Olive. This has nothing to do with you. Her business is with him. She was always going to return. It was only a matter of when.'

'Do you still have ...?' I ask.

Ned reaches down. He pulls his bag of tricks from beneath his chair and swings it up on the table.

'I never let it out of my sight,' he says.

'So what so we do now?'

'We wait.'

The grandfather clock seems to tick too slowly, every second an eternity in which anything could happen as we sit in the half-light waiting.

'In all those years since that day, I had only one question in my mind,' Ned says.

His rocking chair moves evenly back and forth over the softly creaking floorboards. The effect is as hypnotic as the ticking of the clock, though rather than relax me, it focuses my attention.

'I asked myself,' he continues. 'What would I have done if he had taken Olive?'

I feel instantly ashamed that I had asked Victor to make me like him.

'What was your answer?'

'My answer, Miss O, was to study, to find out if there's any way to make them … better, to find some kind of cure, or whether dispatching them is the only way.'

'And that was how you knew what to bring on that day.'

'Yes. But I didn't stop there. I made it my business to know everything I could about them and their ways. There are many different kinds, see? Some are tied to a place, others like to roam. But how ever far they wander, they always come home. And they're superstitious. By no means as superstitious as we are about them, but they like their rituals. And anniversaries.'

'Goodness me. I wish you'd told me all this.'

'Didn't think it right, Miss Olive. I can see that you're still in mourning for Victor, even after these fifty years, so I figured that talking about ways to … how shall I put this? Ways to deal with him, might make you want to open the box, if only to warn him and let him get away somewhere. Not that you would, but they're very persuasive creatures.'

As Ned shares his knowledge with me, the years fall away from him. He is sharp, as he used to be. But I am fully aware this may be because it is tied to the past, and therefore temporary. His confusion when I arrived was plain to see, and nothing to do with whether or not he'd dozed off earlier. How long do I have with you, old friend?

'The parish records don't go back far enough to pinpoint her true beginnings,' Ned continues, 'But I found enough to confirm Victor's story. The death certificates of his wife and daughter gave the causes as "Exsanguination". Now, I know that could be from a number of things, not least knife wounds. When a wife and child die from knife wounds, the first suspect is usually the husband, so I looked further afield to see if there was any kind of police enquiry.'

'You found none?'

'I did not. So I'm guessing the authorities knew the real reason for the deaths, dealt with it as prescribed, and hushed it all up.'

'That's quite a leap of an explanation for an incident that happened so long ago, especially when the records appear to be incomplete.'

'That's exactly what I thought myself. So I looked at what happened more recently. One hundred years ago, to be precise. Several recorded deaths of exsanguination, and no investigations. And what's more. There was an eclipse at that time too.'

'You certainly seem to have worked it all out, Ned.'

'Not all. But enough to …'

He is interrupted by a knock on the door. We look at each other.

'Who is it?' Ned shouts.

He rises slowly from his rocking chair.

'It's me, Grandad,' a voice calls.

Eddie. Or is it? How can we know? Ned is quick on the uptake.

'You'll have to let yourself in lad,' he says.

'I know,' Eddie replies. 'I've got the key, but you'll have to undo the bolts.'

I glance at Ned, and he nods. I move tentatively towards the door and gently pull back the bolts.

'Are you in there too, Miss Hawthorne?' Eddie asks.

'Yes, I am.'

'Don't invite me in! Stand back …'

I take a few paces back towards Ned, and Eddie opens the door. He pushes it wide and glances around the room before entering.

'You two alone here?' Eddie asks.

'We are,' I reply

'Good. I was afraid she might have got here before me.'

'You know about her …?'

'Oh, aye, Miss Hawthorne. I remember Grandad's stories from when I was a little 'un. I know he's not been the same since Nanna died, but he hasn't lost it quite yet.'

'You're doing it again,' Ned huffs. 'Talking about me as if I'm not here.'

'Sorry, Grandad. Got the bag?'

'On the table.' Ned jerks his head in its direction.

Eddie opens it and checks the contents.

'All there, good.'

'But how …?' I must admit, I am still perplexed by Eddie's sudden appearance.

'She's booked rooms in The Cloven Hoof. She wasn't due to arrive until later tonight, but I guess she couldn't wait.' Eddie nods towards the window, indicating the unnatural nightfall. 'I don't know how she's done it. It's not a second eclipse, as far as I can tell. Perhaps it's an illusion just for us, but I'm not taking any chances as to whether she can safely walk about at this hour.'

Eddie slings the bag over his shoulder. He is so like Ned.

'Best bolt the door behind me,' he says as he makes to leave.

'Where do you think you're going, lad?' Ned says. 'Do you know how long I've been waiting for this moment? I'll be damned if you're going to have all the fun without me.'

'Count me in, too.' I link arms with Ned.

And so we step out into this untimely night. The wind is stronger still and threatens to force us off the path. We hold tightly to each other as we walk together, three abreast, considerably more slowly than Eddie would have done alone, even with this wind to fight.

'The day's come at last, eh, Grandad?' Eddie says.

'I've waited my whole life for this. I thought my madness would overtake me before this day arrived.'

'No madness, just … bad luck,' Eddie sighs.

He is resigned to losing his grandfather to this horrible illness. I am still struggling to accept it as his fate.

'We must take care …' I begin, but Ned interrupts me.

'*You* must take care, Olive. Eddie too. You're both still needed here. I'm content to go out with a bang, if need be.'

'Dear Ned. Let's hope it won't come to that.'

Both men look at me sadly, almost pitying my naive optimism.

'We'll cut through the cemetery,' Eddie raises his voice to cut through the deafening wind. Our faces are turned towards the ground in a vain attempt to keep the swirling dust out of our eyes. 'There's something I want to show you.'

He leads us to the old part of the cemetery. It hasn't been used in years. Even the newest headstones date back to before the 1800s. As we pass them, I note the dates stretch further back in time the deeper we go. The graves are overgrown, which is only to be expected, but then I notice something quite strange. One of the graves, right at the far edge of the area, appears to have been tended to recently.

'Someone's been here,' I say to Eddie. 'They've cut away the weeds.'

'That's what I thought at first. But have a closer look, Miss Hawthorne.'

I approach the grave, still holding onto the arms of Eddie and Ned, and I see. The ground has not been tended, rather it is tainted. Nothing can grow there. All greenery stops short a few inches from it, and the edges of the grass that touch its border are withered and black.

'I checked the old maps of the area. This grave lies outside of the cemetery's boundary,' Eddie says. 'And see what's engraved on the headstone …'

He leans forward and wipes dirt away from the worn lettering. The name is hard to read, but I can just make it out: Lily Archer. A name so improbably small and ordinary for one who trails so much darkness in her wake.

'I'm not saying it's definitely her,' Eddie continues. 'But here …' He reads aloud the inscription. *'Once our darling daughter, now far beyond the reach of God.* That's a very strange thing to have on a headstone.'

'We should protect the area,' I say.

'On it, Miss H.'

Eddie reaches into his bag and pulls out a pouch of salt and a bottle of holy water. He sprinkles the salt in a circle around the grave, then throws the holy water at it, first in the shape of a pentagram, then in the sign of the cross.

'The old ways are often the best, but it pays to be sure,' he says.

I am worried that the howling wind will blow the charmed circle away, but my fears are unfounded. Eddie performs his ritual gestures over the consecrated ground and I see that the wind cannot harm the circle: there is an area some six inches above and around the salt that cannot be touched by hand nor element.

'My goodness, you're a skilled Magus,' I say. 'Who taught you this?'

'He did,' Eddie nods towards his grandfather. 'But he doesn't always remember. Keeps telling me he has secrets and skills to teach me someday, even though I started learning at his knee before I could even read. Then sometimes it all comes back to him, and he reminds me I must always be prepared.'

He sighs heavily. We both feel the same about Ned's memory loss: nothing can be done, we must accept it.

The wind whirls even more fiercely, then stops abruptly. Is it too much to hope that Eddie's magic has called it off? Ned looks up and turns his head, as if in the direction of a sound that neither Eddie nor I noticed.

'She's coming,' he says.

The darkness thickens and becomes almost palpable. I can see little more than a few feet in front of me and I can barely move. I hold Ned's and Eddie's arms tightly. Ahead of us, I can just make out the Moon, though it is blurred, and shaped more like a star. Five points cut through this premature night, twisting, curving, growing. Is it growing, or moving closer? Four of the star's points narrow and become limbs, the fifth spirals into the black sky like a bride's veil snatched up by a hurricane. But wait … not 'like', it *is* a veil. A veil that barely covers the white-blonde hair flowing beneath it. She is wearing a wedding dress.

'It's her!' Ned shouts, and my blood runs cold.

I grip my companions' arms so hard, my knuckles turn white. She glides towards us and stops short a few yards away.

And then …

Then, she looks at me, and there is pain and confusion on her face. She knows she cannot return to her grave now Eddie has sealed it, but it's more than that: she wants to communicate with me. For a moment, I see not an evil, undead creature, but a young woman who has carried an awful burden for centuries. I move to reach out to her, but Ned and Eddie hold me back.

'Don't fall for it, Olive,' Ned says. 'It will be a trick. It always is.'

But I am not so sure. Everyone has a tale to tell. I listened to Victor's, now I must listen to hers.

'Tell me!' I call to her. 'Tell me how I can help you.'

Lilyana hangs in the air. Her dress and veil swirl around her as if she were underwater.

'Careful, Miss H,' Eddie takes a step forward and shields me with his body.

'Let me listen to her,' I say. 'Don't let me go to her, but let me listen.'

'She wants you to open your treasure chest, I know it.' Ned says.

'Are you Lily?' I ask her. We know this is her grave, but she must confirm it.

She covers her face with her hands, as though weeping, and nods her head.

'We cannot let you go back. You understand, don't you?'

She nods again.

'Tell me how Lily came to be Lilyana.'

She looks at me for a long time, and then shapes fill my head and everything else disappears.

It's like I am somewhere else. Somewhere indistinct; although I know it is Devil's End. Nothing is clear; all is impressions, hints, feelings. Is this because Lilyana doesn't remember being Lily well enough, or is it that our connection is not strong? No matter. I must try to decipher what she is trying to tell me.

I am Lily, I am Lily, I am Lily.

The words bounce around my skull like an echo in a cathedral. Is she trying to convince me, or herself?

Who is Lilyana? I send this thought to her.

He made her. He lied. He never loved me. All was illusion.

Who is he? The moment I shape this thought, her answer comes to me as if I had thought it myself.

A nobleman from a kingdom in Eastern Europe … Oh, how sadly familiar. He charmed her, promised he would marry her and take her to live with him in his castle. A half-truth. He took her lifeblood and her name. He ferried her many hundreds of miles away from her family and made her lure people to his cold, dank castle for them both to feed on. Decades passed. She grew accustomed to this way of life, but the resentment she harboured towards her creator increased. So she tricked him into walking in daylight during an eclipse, and he was destroyed. At first she felt free, until she realised that she had condemned herself to an eternity alone.

Is this where Victor got the idea? The roots of this story are deep. How far back would we have to search to find a beginning?

I am suddenly aware of a buffeting wind clawing at my clothes and hair, and of Ned and Eddie at my sides.

Lilyana still hangs in the air, her expression sly, all pretence of innocence gone. The sympathy I have for Lily must not be extended to Lilyana. Poor Lily is dead; that we stand by her grave is proof of this. This creature before us is not her. It is a soulless shell, and if we let it return to the grave, it will haunt Devil's End forever more. This must end here.

I fear Lilyana has picked up on my thoughts, for her face changes, and once again I see the sweet, wounded countenance of Lily. But is it a trick? Or could it be …

The wind drops to a breeze, and the air feels warmer. A look of panic crosses Lilyana's face, then her features relax and she – Lily – is almost beatific.

'Look at the sky!' Ned shouts. 'Get ready, lad.'

I tear my gaze away from the woman and glance up. The black night has already warmed to violet, which in turn is scratched away by fingers of pink and gold, and finally …

Blue.

The day has returned, and with it a fierce Sun. Lilyana shrieks. The sound rips through me like a knife. She throws up her hands to shade herself, but to no avail. Her white skin chars and smoulders and falls from her bones, which, now exposed, turn to ash.

'Now, lad, now!' Ned calls to Eddie.

The two men let go of my arms. Eddie rushes forward and empties the contents of his bag onto the ground. He sweeps up Lilyana's remains with his grandfather's hearth set, and pours them into an ornately carved silver box, almost identical to the one that houses Victor.

'Now you seal it up good, lad,' Ned says. 'Use wax and the charms I taught you.'

'We did it,' Eddie says. 'We did it.'

It would have been churlish to point out that it was Lily who did it, or at least the part of her that remained within Lilyana. But then I notice he is addressing the grave, in acknowledgement that Lily had indeed laid her own soul to rest. He is wise, this young man.

'Right, let's get you two home.' Eddie gathers up his things, and we all link arms once more.

We walk home as the Sun prepares to set in a sky daubed with coral-coloured streaks. A sense of peace washes over me, and, I suspect, over my companions also. I cannot say what the future holds for Ned. Only time will tell if his memory problems are due to the stress of his recent bereavement. Surely fate would not be so cruel as to afflict Ned with the same Alzheimer's that took his wife, Sally, just eighteen months ago.

'Well, here we are then,' Eddie says, as we reach the door of my cottage.

'Thank you, Eddie.'

'No, thank you, Miss H. I really appreciate you keeping an eye on Grandad. It's not been easy for him without Nanna.'

'It's always a pleasure to talk over old times with Ned.'

Eddie smiles sadly then takes Ned's arm.

'Come on, Trouble. Let's see how long we can keep you out

of mischief.'

'Less of your lip, my lad,' Ned says with a wink.

And now there are two. Two silver boxes, one in Eddie's care, the other in mine. When my time comes, Victor's box will be passed on to Eddie. Perhaps it is unwise to keep them like this. We know there will always be danger, but silver is a great protector.

The past has been reconciled with the present. For now, at least. Though I am concerned about the repeating patterns and cyclical nature of this tale that seemingly spirals down generations. I need time to process this, and to plan for what must be done when Ned and I are gone and Eddie is left alone with the burden. I hope he will have his own family someday, and that they can be trusted to take up his duties when he is no longer able.

Alas, my dreams of having a family of my own were just that: dreams, fancies, imaginings. Like my love for Victor. No, that was real, albeit … star-crossed, shall we say? Poor Victor. He gave up his existence to protect me. What better example of true love could there be? Perhaps it is wishful thinking, but sometimes I feel him watching over me, his love keeping guard. And I miss him so, but I must remain resolute.

'Well, dear Victor,' I say aloud, as I plant a kiss on the box. 'I suppose it will have to be enough that we had our day in the Sun, just as you wished. Goodnight, my love. Sleep well.'

THE CAT WHO WALKED THROUGH WORLDS
Debbie Bennett

I noticed this morning that Rhad is missing again. I don't know why it upsets me so when he goes. It's not the first time he's done a vanishing act and I know he'll be back eventually; it's just that each time he goes marks another section of my life passing. I picture him back with his family and then I wonder whether he resents the time he spends with me. Maybe I'm just a silly old woman with whom he once had an alliance. And *alliance* is such a strange word for our relationship too – strange, but fitting – as my kind and his could never really be friends.

Rhad is my cat. Well strictly speaking, he's not *my* cat – he's not really anybody's anything, but I like to think we've brought each other some measure of comfort over the years. Truth be told, I do sometimes think he quite enjoys this life; the part of him that is cat has been dominant for so long that it may now be second nature. Yet behind those pale eyes is a deeper intelligence than that of just cat. A fey intelligence. Rhad is so much more than he seems.

Rhadamanthus is his full name. A bit of a mouthful even on a good day, but I have only myself to blame for that. After all, it was I who named him and I've never found out the name he was born with. If indeed he was born at all. I've never asked his name – his true name – nor anything about his former life. I'm not sure I'd like the answers, not given the circumstances under which we became companions. And it's not like we can sit down in the kitchen in front of the Aga with a pot of tea and slice of home-made lemon drizzle cake and have a cosy chat about our lives, is it? I mean he's a *cat*, and while he does indeed enjoy curling up next to the Aga, he doesn't eat cake nor drink tea. Or talk, unfortunately, which is both something of a blessing and a curse. Would I like what he could tell me?

I first met him in different form when I was looking for early windfalls in the tiny orchard next to the barn. I can't really say human because I don't think he was. Back then, there was something about him, something in the way he moved and spoke, the way the very air around him seemed to make space for his form. And it wasn't the first time I'd encountered his people.

There had been a storm the previous night. Late summer wind and rain had ripped through my small-holding, and I remember lying awake in bed wondering why the Earth seemed so badly off-balance this year and what I could do to fix it. Beneath the drumming of the rain on the porch, I heard the plonk-plonk of apples dropping onto the tin roof of the lean-to adjacent to the barn, closely followed by the rattle and crash of a slate falling from the porch roof. I sighed, wondering where I was going to find the money for repairs and whether there would be a puddle on the floor by tomorrow morning. Eventually I fell asleep dreaming of water, rivers and oceans in faraway places, of mermaids and sirens, beauty and danger in equal measure. I wonder now if that was an omen, a portent of things to come – my subconscious has always been one step ahead of me, as if it likes to let me gently acclimatise to a new situation before my conscious mind has to deal with it. I've learned to trust it over the years and it's never yet let me down.

The following morning, the wind had stilled. The sky was a misty pale blue and the air felt clean and fresh and full of possibilities. I pulled on a pair of old gardening boots and went outside to inspect the damage. At the front of the house, there were two slates sticking out of the grass at odd angles like vandalised tombstones. I pulled them out carefully, grateful that at least they were unbroken, and thought to store them in the barn around the back of the house until I could find someone to fix them for me. A quick look at the porch roof showed no serious damage and there was no apparent urgency.

I picked my way through the fallen apples to the barn, kicking a few out of my way so that the door opened. I've never much liked the barn – it's always seemed slightly creepy, slightly *otherworldly*, as if it had once been used for less mundane things than storing gardening tools and hay for the neighbour's ponies who graze the paddock behind. I had cast a cleansing spell when I first inherited Devil's End. A protection ward followed, and for a time the place felt clean but the spell wears thin over time and needed replacing here far more often than anywhere else.

I left the slates on the workbench underneath the window and went back outside with a bucket, thinking to pick up the fallen fruit and make use of it somehow – and that's when I heard it. The sound of scuffling coming from the paddock on the other side of the orchard wall. Fabric tearing on rough brickwork. I heard someone climbing, and I knew I wasn't alone.

I'm not a nervous person. I don't scare easily. In my line of work, I'm prepared for most eventualities and I knew if I screamed, the locals would come running. The post-office is only a few doors away and there are always people coming and going along the lane – the village centre is less than quarter of a mile away and sometimes on a clear summer night I can hear people in the pub garden, or sitting on the benches on the green.

So I stood my ground in my orchard, hand on hip, waiting for the intruder to show themselves. If he or she thought to burgle my little cottage, they'd find nothing of value anyway, but they wouldn't get that far. I can defend myself. I've had years of practice.

And then I saw a figure scrambling over the top of the orchard wall and onto the roof of the lean-to next to the barn. He looked like an oddly-dressed youth of maybe seventeen – not a child but not yet fully grown into his body. Blond hair curled halfway down his back but there was nothing feminine about him. Over the top of a dark tunic, he carried a large tatty satchel and as I watched from below, he stretched towards the overhanging tree and in one fluid movement had an apple secured and placed in the satchel. He hadn't seen me yet.

'Good morning,' I said loudly.

He almost fell off the roof but recovered himself quickly with a smile as he turned to face me. 'Your pardon, mistress. I was –'

'I can see what you were doing,' I retorted, perhaps unnecessarily harsh. 'Stealing my apples.'

'Apples,' he agreed, grinning widely. He took another one, balanced effortlessly on one foot on the mossy roof.

'My apples,' I said. 'And anyway, they're not ripe yet.'

'You're picking them.' He pointed to the bucket.

'They're my apples. I can pick them as I choose.' I softened slightly. 'And I'm only collecting windfalls. Not much good for eating, but they'll do very nicely for green apple jelly for the village fête.'

'Windfalls,' he repeated. I wondered if he was simple. He slithered down the roof and jumped to the ground. My neck prickled as a cloud covered the sun. There was something about him, something in those guileless eyes that was far older than he seemed to be, and as he stood in front of me, I shivered.

He seemed to take pity on me, then as we studied each other. 'Do not be afraid,' he said softly, touching my arm. 'There are those that would do you harm, but I am not one of them.' Our eyes met for a moment and then he shook his head and stepped away, grinning again. He opened the satchel, took out the two apples and offered them to me in one hand, bowing with mock formality. 'Your apples, mistress. I am truly sorry for my crime.'

It wasn't much of an apology – I could hear the humour in his voice. 'Keep them.' I pointed to the rest of the fruit around the base of the tree. 'Take what you need. I have more than enough for myself,' I added, as he filled the satchel.

He stood, satchel full, and stared at me again, head cocked slightly to one side as if he was seeing something that I could not. Then he took my hand, raised it to his lips and kissed it, before leaping for the wall at the back of the orchard. At the top, he paused for a second and turning back called out: 'Good fortune go with you, my lady Olive!' And then he was gone and my hand burned with his kiss.

I didn't see him again for many weeks. Occasionally I would leave a few apples out by the barn, maybe milk or a couple of fresh eggs, when I had some left over. In return I found the slates on the porch mysteriously mended one morning, and the fox that had been bothering the chickens never returned. The windfalls were often stacked in neat piles against the barn wall and the blight on the tree itself healed. The apples were bigger and better than previous harvests. But I never saw my apple thief. Not until the children disappeared.

It was a quiet autumn, all things considered. *Samhain* came and went without incident, which surprised me. The cross-quarter days are generally when the barriers between the worlds are at their most delicate, and I had half-expected to see my *sídhe* friend – for I was certain he was one of the folk – but the orchard was quiet, apart from the sounds of the village children trick-or-treating. They never come here, and I've never been sure whether that's a mark of respect, or whether their parents are genuinely scared of me at that time of year. When one has a reputation as a witch of any colour or persuasion, then Hallowe'en is probably not a good time to receive visitors. Sometimes I'm not sure whether to laugh or cry myself, and I've always kept a bowl of sweets by the front door just in case; I imagine they'd never dare to trick me, but the treats remain unclaimed.

That *Samhain*, I left a home-made pie in the barn. An apple pie, as I thought he'd appreciate the irony. It was gone by morning, the foil tray left behind all clean and shiny as if it had never been used. The day after, there was a stone flagon in its place. When I pulled the stopper, a pungent aroma filled the barn – spices and fruit and strange scents that sat on the back of the tongue and tasted of eternity – and I knew that however freely this gift had been given, I dare not let it touch my lips. Not even my apple thief was above the laws of the land, whichever land this had been sent from, although if I could have but just one taste, I was sure it would be better than the sweetest wine. A sip of paradise might be enough for the rest of my life.

However long that might be.

I resealed the flagon, the scent vanishing instantly, and I leaned back against the workbench, breathless. 'I'm sorry,' I said to the empty barn. 'I dare not.'

You are wise, the silence said to me, *beyond mortal years*. The temperature dropped sharply and goosebumps broke out on my skin. Unprepared, I gripped the edge of the workbench, but the silence lengthened until it was broken by a mouse scurrying across the floor. A door banged somewhere, the temperature rose again and whatever had happened was over.

The following day was grey and muddy, the kind of day when the air seems to swallow sound, and I'd been working on cleansing and preparing the cottage for winter, collecting wood from the copse at the back of the paddock both for burning in the fire and for the making of charms. I was stacking wood by the barn, from where one of the local lads would chop it into logs to fit into the wood-burner. Charlie was fifteen, but stronger than he looked. I used to pay him in home-made cider, and I'm quite sure his parents didn't approve of the arrangement but it suited us both well-enough. He's married now, with children of his own.

As I finished off my woodpile, I heard muffled voices on the lane, deadened by the damp air. Sounds of crying – one, no, *two* people heading in my direction as they stopped by my gate.

'The police will find them, Annalise.'

Annalise. Such a pretty name. That would be Lucy's mum, which meant that the speaker was probably Abby's mum. I'd known Annalise for a few years – her daughter was eight or nine and quite the sweetest of girls. She reminded me so much of Poppy at that age. Abby and her family were new to the village; there were two boys and a girl – all redheads with tempers to match and constantly squabbling in the way that only siblings do.

What was Abby's mum's name? I was racking my brains as the two women appeared on my driveway, Annalise hanging back, but urged onwards by … by … Caroline? No – *Kathy*. That was it. Kathy.

I wiped my hands on my trousers and went forwards to meet them. Both women had red eyes and Annalise was trying hard not to sniff.

'Are you Olive?' asked Kathy.

Annalise nudged her. 'Olive's lived here *forever*, Kath. She can find the girls, I know she can.'

Find the girls? 'What's happened?' I asked, concerned now. 'Are Lucy and Abby hiding out on you again?' They'd played this game of hide-and-seek many times over the summer in the churchyard, popping out at inopportune moments and scaring visitors.

But this seemed more serious, somehow. Not just childish games. And I'd heard Kathy mention the police.

Annalise blew her nose. 'The girls have vanished, Olive. They didn't come back from school yesterday, although their friends say they got on the bus as normal.'

'Abby was going to Lucy's straight from school for tea,' Kathy added. 'I didn't even know there was anything wrong until Annalise called me to ask if perhaps they'd come to mine instead.'

'But they were on the bus!' Annalise wailed. 'They're nine years old! I only started letting Lucy walk back from the bus-stop without me when Abby moved in. They were only allowed to walk together. Never alone. So where are they? They were on the bus!' she repeated.

'I know. I saw them pass the house.' The bus stop was just up the lane from my cottage and I remembered seeing the two of them pass my gate arm-in-arm as I was on my way to the barn. Just before I'd found the flagon.

Had I been meant to drink the wine? *Faery wine?* Would I have forgotten what I'd seen? I didn't like the dark path down which I was headed, but there was one way to find out for sure.

'Will you help us?' Kathy asked. 'Annalise says you can … *find* things. Can you find our girls?'

Many of the villagers said I could find things. Or do things.

Very few would actually call me a witch – at least not to my face – but most of them probably thought it, even if they didn't quite believe what they were thinking. There are no witches in 21st century England, if there ever were any at all.

'Come inside, both of you.' I glanced around the orchard, not sure what I was looking for. It was beginning to get dark.

Inside, I ushered them into the sitting room and left them with a box of tissues while I set the kettle to boil and fetched the things I'd need. Back in the sitting room I placed a small table in the centre of the rug; on top of that went a large ceramic bowl full of water. A few drops of olive oil followed and I was ready.

Kathy looked at me dubiously. 'If you really are … what they say you are … don't you need something a bit more … *elaborate*?'

'Pfft.' I knelt on the floor by the bowl. 'It's what is within that counts. All the rest is simply for effect. Do you have something of Lucy's?' I asked Annalise. 'I've known her since she was a little girl and it will be easier to connect with her.'

Lucy's mother handed me a small stuffed animal. I wondered if she'd brought it with her simply for comfort – or whether she'd known what I needed. In all the best stories, they always need something belonging to the victim, if only to give the dog a scent to follow.

I studied the toy rabbit. It was a shade of grey that had once been pale blue and was now simply well-loved. Two button eyes looked at me and I wondered what they saw. A witch? Or just a woman with some skills that were still occasionally needed – even in 21st century England.

The rabbit grew warm in my hand. I placed in on the table next to the bowl and swirled my fingers quickly in the water. The oil broke up, made shapes on the surface and –

– Lucy and Abby are walking down the lane, arm in arm and giggling over some silly joke. Lucy's wearing a red scarf, a present from her uncle for her birthday, and Abby twines it around her own neck too. The focus narrows, the world around them stills and they hesitate as if they can sense something is not quite right. A mist swirls and as it clears, the lane is gone. It's hard dry earth under their sensible school

shoes and high hedges either side of the track.

And now there are footsteps. Hoofbeats, but no horses, and unseen animals pace the girls who are running. The scarf falls to the ground, forgotten. As the girls run, the hoofbeats are louder, faster. Lucy is crying and Abby trips and lands heavily on the track; she looks back and screams.

Behind her stands a boy with hair like spun gold.
Apple thief.
And he smiles that fey smile, and –

– I shook my head, breaking out of the trance to see Annalise and Kathy watching me. As I stood up, I unclenched my fists to see I'd drawn blood in the palm of my left hand. Before I stopped to think about what I was doing, I held my hand over the bowl and let a single drop fall onto the surface. Blood magic is always stronger than a simple scrying, and blood spilled by ritual is the strongest of all.

Annalise let out a tiny gasp and I looked down to see the water in the bowl swirl rapidly, turn black and then just as quickly clear again.

'What was …?' She trailed off, not wanting to finish the question. Maybe she just didn't want to know the answer – that others had taken the girls beyond this world and I wasn't sure where, or if they would ever come back again.

Later, after I had done my best to reassure Annalise and Kathy that the girls were fine and would be home soon, I stood in the centre of the barn, remembering something from my childhood. The gypsy's comment: *Sacrifices may have to be made.* But not children, surely? Was it not enough that my Poppy had disappeared? I was lying to the women. They were good people – decent people – and I was simply pretending everything was going to be all right, when in reality I was out of my depth and I knew it.

I felt betrayed.

'Why?' I cried out. 'And why you?'

We'd had an understanding, I was sure we had, my apple thief and I. Mutual respect – of his ways and mine – and although I was fairly sure he had far greater powers at his command than I, he had seemed genuine on the one occasion we had met. It just went to prove that you can't trust the fey folk, no matter what they might say or do. I should have learned that much by now.

I couldn't stop thinking about him, the boy with the golden hair. My apple thief. And as the night drew in, so did time. All evening, it seemed that every moment was staged, every action a prelude to what would surely come next, as if I was playing a part in a play but couldn't step off the stage nor bring down the curtain. I knew I was being watched, but by who, or what, I had no idea.

I went to bed early, knowing that I wouldn't get much sleep that night and it seemed prudent to take my rest where I could. And yet I fell asleep quickly, the world collapsing in on itself until –

– Lucy and Abby are playing on a swing. A rough plank of wood suspended by what looks like vines or creepers from a huge tree, so tall that the top is in the clouds. Its branches are vast, creating cathedral-like canopies over the forest floor, and its roots are the size of trees themselves, protruding from the earth and leaving chasms underneath where whole armies might lie sleeping, knights on white steeds awaiting an age that may never come again. This may be the only tree that ever was or ever will be.

But Lucy and Abby are unaware of the oddness of their surroundings. Gone is the terror of the chase, the fear of the unknown. They take it in turns on the swing, pushed by a bright creature dressed in green, who appears barely human, although she wears Lucy's red scarf around her neck. She sniffs it every now and again, inhaling the scent, and picks off a hair which she examines on the palm of her hand before blowing it gently onto the breeze.

Lucy shrieks with laughter and Abby cries that it's her turn now. Lucy skids to a stop, jumps off and lets Abby take her place. Lucy ducks away from the swing and runs over to the boy with the hair like spun gold.

He's sitting on a tree root, arms clasped around one knee.
Apple thief.
He pats Lucy's shoulder absently, the way a father might pat a small child, but his attention is elsewhere, in another world entirely, and –

– I woke abruptly. He was here, I knew he was, and I dressed as fast as I could, stumbling in the darkness of the bedroom. I've never felt the presence of other worlds as strongly as I did that night. Liminal spaces and times exist everywhere and everywhen, but that night Devil's End was in a dimension all of its own. Downstairs in the kitchen, I grabbed my pouch from the back of the door, sensing I might need weapons to deal with whatever was out there. The grimoire was on the kitchen table and I placed my palm on it, drawing support from its presence, but I left it where it was.

How could I have got it so wrong? My apple thief had been stealing from me when we had first met, but I've always prided myself on being a good judge of character. Maybe I was fooling myself as much as everyone else.

Outside, the night was still. Not a breath of wind stirred the trees in the orchard. The moon was full and round, and yet it had been but a quarter the previous day. And the shadows were … wrong, somehow. Elongated and out of kilter with the moon's place in a black and starless sky. I shivered. Liminal spaces indeed.

I twisted to look behind me at the cottage. Devil's End was still there, still solid and welcoming, but if I went back inside and closed the door, it would doubtless be a different night outside, should I ever dare to open it again.

And he was there, my apple thief, standing ankle-deep in a patch of moonlight that rippled gently across the rough orchard grass. He looked older tonight and his eyes glittered. Gone was the boyish smirk he had worn last time and there was no smile on his face now.

'You are right to be concerned,' he said, all traces of gaiety gone from his voice.

'It was you.' My affection for him had changed. This was no boy stealing apples anymore. This was a man. Stealing children.

He nodded, as if reading my thoughts. 'Come,' he said. 'There is little time and much to be done.'

And he strode towards the barn, the curious patch of moonlight moving with him like a stage spotlight. I followed – how could I not? Though a part of me wanted to run, cast a protection spell and bury my head under its covers until daylight came, I knew I had to see it through. This was why I was here, why I had always been here, to protect this world from outside interference. Abby and Lucy were my responsibility.

The barn door didn't so much open at his touch, as at his gesture. A wave of his hand, fingers outstretched, and the door opened smoothly and silently. I hesitated on the boundary, wondering how symbolic a barn door could actually be, and then I stepped over the threshold.

And there in the hay were two small sleeping figures, curled up like sacrifices at a straw altar. Lucy and Abby.

I rushed forwards, but he held out an arm. 'Wait.' He turned to face me. 'You must act quickly and quietly,' he said. 'Do not worry – they will not wake until the morning, when this will all seem as if a dream. I have made it so.'

'You took them.' I confronted him. 'Why? And why bring them back now?'

'Not I,' he said, but he would not meet my eyes. 'You were kind to me and I do not forget. And you were *there* – in the garden – and I know not how that is even possible.' He was looking around nervously, and I wondered who, or what, he was expecting.

'What garden?' And the ultimate question. 'Who *are* you?'

He brushed it off. 'We do not have time for talking,' he replied. 'If you would see the girls returned to their families then you must take them. Now.'

I bent to pick up Lucy, then stood up, arms empty as I heard another voice. In the doorway of the barn stood a figure, silhouetted in the moonlight. Tall and slim, he had an aura that would be apparent even to the untrained eye – to one such as myself, his presence was overpowering and I found it hard to keep my balance as I reached behind me for support. My fingers curled around a pitchfork as I realised I might have to fight for my own survival, as well as Lucy and Abby. The grimoire could not help me here.

'You!' The stranger pointed at my apple thief. 'You will regret your actions tonight, boy. I will deal with you.'

'My lord,' he said softly, staring at the ground. I was beginning to realise he had risked a lot to return the children to me. He was as scared of this creature as I was, and the thought did not fill me with confidence. But I had to protect the girls: I may have been unable to save my Poppy, but I would not fail Lucy and Abby.

I could feel the stranger's aura stretch cold fingers in my direction. 'And as for *you*, hawthorn woman, Huath, Queen of May – it is you who stands in our way in this place; you who holds the door closed to us. Only you. But it is no longer your time and space. *Beltàin* is long past, the year ends and you are no more than mortal. You will not oppose me.'

And he dismissed me as something unworthy of his attention, of so little significance that he didn't need to concern himself further beyond that warning. He waved at the faery youth instead. 'Go.'

My apple thief hesitated. I could see his indecision in the set of his shoulders, the tension in his hands as he flexed his fingers gently. Then he turned towards the barn door, still with his head lowered. There would be no more help here and I didn't blame him, not really.

I peered into the depths of the barn, beyond where the girls lay sleeping. It seemed that there were other things there now – faces floating in the darkness, whispers on the night air. Shadows crept out from the corners towards the sleeping children. I stepped forwards with my pitchfork, wondering if the old tales were true and fey folk were indeed unable to tolerate cold iron.

The barn seemed to get darker still as the shadows

smothered the bundles on the hay and the shapes resolved into figures taking form; smoke-skinned and blood-eyed, they scooped up the children but I couldn't let them go. Not without a fight.

I plunged the pitchfork at the nearest shadow-figure and it squealed. But the fork left my hand as if grabbed by an unseen force and it flew across the barn, the tines embedding deep into the back wall.

I ran towards the girls, who were already fading into the blackness at the end of the barn. The shadow-creatures swarmed around me and I could feel tiny fingernails – or were they teeth? – digging into the soft flesh of my upper arms. Fingers moved through my clothing and there were high-pitched shrieks as they touched the pouch at my waist. I could smell burning as I smacked them away and reached for Lucy's dangling arm, holding on to her hand and refusing to let go.

A wave of dizziness, and darkness turned abruptly to sunlight. Screwing up my eyes against the glare, I was still holding Lucy's hand as I realised I was sitting on wet grass, Lucy lying next to me and Abby nearby. The shadow-creatures had gone and indeed there was no place for shadows in a world this brilliant. Everything seemed brighter and sharper – the grass was greener, the sky was bluer and the air crisp and cold, despite the sunlight.

Sometimes I can't remember how many years I've been the steward of Devil's End. Sometimes I feel like I've lived several lifetimes and I long for rest, for sleep and maybe one day for peace. But back then, in that place, I felt more alive – more *complete* – than I'd felt in a long time. There had never been more possibilities than there were at that moment.

Or more danger.

My right hand was wet from the grass. The moisture sparkled like champagne on my fingers and I had an urge to touch my lips and taste the dew, but even that small infraction might cost too much, so I wiped my hand on my sleeve instead and wondered what I could do now. I was on the edge of a forest. Behind me the treeline thickened quickly and there was no path through that I could see. In front, the ground dropped away sharply to a view that wouldn't have been out of place in a Disney movie – gentle green rolling hills led to snow-capped mountains in the distance. There was no sign of civilisation and no way back to Devil's End. I was trapped.

Trying not to panic, I heard a rustle behind me and two figures stepped out of the trees. My apple thief clasped his hands in front of him, head bowed, but his master ignored him, striding over as I scrambled to my feet and stood in front of the girls, my arms outstretched as if I thought I could form some kind of protective shield.

He laughed, then looked at me strangely, lips pursed. 'You have more power than I expected, May Queen. Use it wisely.'

He was looking at my left hand. A speck of red at the centre of my palm – the cut I'd made whilst scrying – and the blood droplet crawled across my skin and beaded by my little finger. I raised my hand and licked the blood before it could fall. The taste was salty and rich and it was an effort to not keep sucking. I was feeling dizzy with this world, dizzy with the power that I could feel in the earth.

'Wise woman. Your thorns are sharp.' He laughed again. 'But you are too late. You have already spilled blood; I can smell it in the earth. You are already connected to the land, and that makes you mine to command.'

The blood I'd dripped while scrying had opened this world up to me. And me to it. But maybe I could use it to my advantage. At least I didn't appear to be beneath his notice now. 'What price the girls?' I asked, affecting a confidence I didn't feel.

'No price,' he replied. 'They are not yours to bargain. Nor mine either.'

'Then whose?'

'That is not your business. You amuse me, May Queen, with your pathetic human attempts to barter. Do not anger me and I may yet let you leave my lands.'

'I'm not leaving without Lucy and Abby.'

'Then stay.' His voice was casual. 'It matters not to me. You might indeed enjoy my kingdom. But now,' he said, turning away, 'I have other matters to deal with and I do not tolerate disobedience.'

But my apple thief had edged his way back to the tree line and now he was staring at something with a look of horror on his face.

'What is it, boy?' He hesitated. 'How can this be?'

Embedded into the trunk of one of the trees was my old pitchfork, the one I'd hurled at the shadow-creatures in the barn and thrown across into another world. Steel tines, iron-strong, and maybe there was something in the old stories, because the tree was shaking softly, small spots of *nothingness* appearing on its trunk.

The pitchfork fell out, but the spots got bigger, merging together into a black hole of *absence* where the tree trunk had been.

'Witch-woman, this is your doing. What evils have you unleashed?'

'My magic may be as strong as yours, *my lord*,' I said with a touch of sarcasm, as I reached into my pouch. I'd been cutting wood all week, making charms each evening. Three twigs – fresh-cut and fragrant – one each of oak and ash and hawthorn tied with a red cord. Oak and thorn for protection; ash for the world-tree, and fire signs all of them. *Dair, nuin* and *sceach* worked in ritual over many nights.

It would be enough. It would have to be enough. Blood, iron and witch-magic. And here I suspected my magic would be stronger than Devil's End – here where the world-tree's roots grew strong and there was magic in the land itself. Quickly I broke each twig in two, unwound the binding of the cord and made two new bundles.

He hadn't seen me yet, too concerned with the unmaking of the space around the tree. I wondered how far it would spread, this iron disease – whether it could eat away a whole world like a cancer. It didn't seem fair and I didn't want to destroy anything, just keep myself and the girls safe and get us home.

But my movements caught his eye as I knelt and tucked a

twig bundle into Lucy's shirt and pressed it close to her chest, whispering a few words of protection. I did the same for Abby and as I stood up, he strode back towards me, power emanating from his entire being with such force that I staggered under its onslaught.

The girls were stirring, whatever spell was upon them faltering under the charms. The dark lord's eyes blazed with anger and he pointed a finger at me.

'You dare to stand against me, witch-woman? So be it.'

I had nothing left. Without the protection of my charms, I could feel my mind slipping under the weight of his rage and his sheer presence. I couldn't move, couldn't even avert my eyes from his face as he held my gaze and showed me a darkness I never wanted to admit existed. A cold numbness crept into my body and I knew I had failed. Failed to save the girls and failed to protect Devil's End. Would I ever see my home again?

But a movement behind the dark lord caught my attention as I fought his hold over me. My apple thief was running, darting underneath his master's arm. Reaching down to the girls, he snatched the two twig bundles and threw one back at me. 'Save yourself,' he said. 'Take one child. I will bring the other.'

As the twigs touched my body, the spell broke and I tucked the charm into my collar. Picking up Lucy, I watched as he tossed the other charm at his master with a sharp cry in a strange tongue. As the charm touched the dark lord, the air swirled, a vortex of fire around the figure in front of me, and I could feel the roar of anger turn to pain, feel the heat of the flames. How could a simple protection-charm do that, even in this world? It wasn't possible.

'The magic is indeed yours, Mistress Olive,' said my apple thief, 'but not *all* the power.' He smiled slightly. 'I am not entirely without influence, even under his command.'

The dark lord was ablaze now and he was burning, melting, immolating in bright flames in front of us. And then suddenly he was gone and nothing remained, not even ash on the grass.

'There will be others,' said my apple thief. 'It is but a brief respite. We must hurry.' He winced, screwing up his face in sudden pain as he scooped Abby up in his arms and headed straight for the place where the pitchfork had been.

The entire area shimmered, heat haze over summer tarmac. The pitchfork was gone – the tree was gone – and in its place was nothing, an absence of substance, and so dark it seemed to swallow my vision. A portal? My apple thief barely hesitated before plunging straight into it and so I had no choice but to follow, or risk being stranded here alone and defenceless.

My apple thief's fingers were burned where he'd touched the charms. But his intentions had been good and thus the charm had not harmed him further. Together we took the girls back to their homes – an odd movement of his hands, a couple of words from him in a strange tongue and the parents were happy that their daughters were back from a childish escapade. I wondered how he did that, and whether he would be able to manipulate *my* memories as easily as he could other humans. He had not been completely immune to my magic, so I hoped I would be able to put up some resistance – I needed to remember this encounter, so I could learn from it and be better prepared next time I had dealings with the fey folk.

Back at Devil's End, he didn't take his leave, though I sensed he wanted to flee, but didn't know where to go. Perhaps he was too scared to go home after he had helped me. So I made herbal tea and applied a poultice to his burns, while he watched me, wide-eyed and silent as I chattered inanely, trying to fill the space between us with something, anything, to keep my wits together and process what had happened.

I lit two incense sticks on the mantel and my one-sided conversation dried up. We sat in silence watching the flames of the fire all night until, at dawn, there was a knock at the cottage door.

A woman stood there – young and yet impossibly old at the same time. My apple thief didn't move nor even look at her, but we both knew his fate was about to be decided.

'Judgement has been passed,' she said. 'Stand before your queen.'

He dragged himself to his feet, head bowed once more.

'Be at peace,' she said softly. She leaned forward and kissed his forehead gently. He shuddered, the blisters on his fingers disappearing.

He flexed his hands, looking up at her. 'Lady,' he said, barely above a whisper.

'You have my thanks,' she said. 'Nevertheless, you may not return,' she told him. 'And yet you cannot remain here in this world in this human form. You would find it … difficult.' She turned to me. 'Mistress Whitethorn. Guardian of this place. You seem in need of a familiar.'

'A cat?' I'd had many cats and none had been good for much other than keeping the mice from the barn.

'Not just any cat. A companion, perhaps, in feline form. Who may have leave to go back to his people once every seven years, for such time as may appear decent in this world and ours.'

My apple thief said nothing. I wasn't sure if this was reward or punishment.

'You have the right to name your familiar,' she continued.

He had killed one of his own – betrayed his people. And yet he had done it to save others not of his kind. My apple thief had both judged and been judged. The power of life and death was not one to be taken lightly.

'Rhadamanthus,' I said.

And that was it. He was named – no longer my apple thief, but one who sat in judgement of the dead. It seemed fitting. He left the cottage without a word and I never heard him speak again nor saw him in that form. Later that day, I went outside to hang some washing and there he was, a sleek young tortie cat sitting on the orchard wall and staring at me in a way that only cats can do.

I admit it was awkward at first. He would be curled up on my bed and I'd want to get changed or have a bath. And I had to remember he could understand human speech and was quite capable of doing what I asked – even if he did have a mind of his own and frequently ignored my request. Oh, yes – I got very used to Rhad's looks. I would be telling him something that had happened that day and he would stare at me, head cocked slightly to one side and an expression which clearly told me I was talking too much and he really wasn't that interested. Who needed words?

But we got on well enough and developed a healthy respect for one another. Being who he was, of course, Rhad had other abilities. I remember a time when he spent most of a week roaming around the village green and hissing at anyone who came close to him or a particular bench. Julie, the post-mistress told me about it first, but when I asked him, he kept turning away and refusing to co-operate. And then, three days later, there was a full moon and he woke me and made me follow him back into the village. By the bench, he raked away some fallen leaves with his paws and helped me dig into a small patch of loose earth. A few inches down we found a hex, crudely carved in wax and buried in the earth. I carried it back to the cottage and disposed of it safely, and I never did find out who – or what – had placed it there, nor what they had intended to happen.

Years passed. Rhad and I got used to each other, until I hardly thought of him as anything other than a cat with special powers and I could barely remember the young fey he had once been. And then one night he curled up on my knee – something he did more for my comfort than his – and the following morning he was nowhere to be seen.

I called for him, searched the barn and the orchard and the sunny spots on the wall where he liked to laze away the days, but there was no sign of him. And I remembered the queen's words – that he would be allowed to return to his own people every seven years. Did Rhadamanthus have a family, I wondered? Did the fey folk even live in groups which we might call family? Were they celebrating his return home? Was Rhad himself celebrating? I pictured him as I had last seen him in human form, barely more than a child, and wondered whether he had aged at all.

And I missed him. Missed his silent company, his ability to sense my moods and yet stop me from taking myself too seriously at times. I missed the way I could tell him all my problems and somehow in the telling of them would come the answers. We were a team, Rhad and I.

Would he come back? Did he want to?

Maybe two months after he'd left, when I'd convinced myself that he had served his time and I would never see him again, there was a knock on the door. It was Saturday afternoon, a few days before *Samhain* and almost seven years since Lucy and Abby had gone missing. The girls had grown up into lovely teenagers; still best friends, they frequently popped over to help out around Devil's End, yet they never spoke of that time and I wasn't sure they even remembered what had happened.

Abby was by far the more practical of the pair – she fully intended to finish her A levels and go off to university to study engineering. But Lucy was given to flights of fancy; she liked her books, had tried her hand at creative writing and would often sit and stare into space dreamily. Rhad had always spent more time with her and I wondered if he was perhaps guarding her in some way I didn't understand.

This particular Saturday, the girls were helping me bake cakes for a party in the village hall that night. I was turning out Victoria sponges onto cake stands and Abby was mixing buttercream, so it was Lucy who answered the door for me.

'Olive, it's the vicar!'

'Come in,' I called to him, putting down the oven gloves door as I turned to the kitchen doorway. Lucy skipped back in, a smug smile on her face, followed by Canon Smallwood, who was carrying a small and rather scruffy white cat wrapped up in an old blanket.

'Miss Hawthorne. I wonder if you'd help me out with a small problem,' he said. 'The girl who cleans the church found this little scrap in the porch this morning. He seems healthy enough, and I was about to take him to the RSPCA when I remembered I'd overheard someone saying you'd recently lost your cat.' The covert look he snuck at Lucy didn't escape my notice.

I had hardly *lost* Rhad, but it didn't seem fair to say that to the vicar or the cat. 'You overheard someone, did you? And would that someone by any chance be a certain Lucy Jones?'

'Might be.' Lucy shrugged. 'Oh, come on, Olive. You know how you miss Rhad. I wonder what happened to him? He always was the oddest of cats – I swear he sometimes knew exactly what I was thinking.'

'Yes, come on, Olive,' Abby joined in, wheedling. 'Rhad's not coming back. He's been gone for too long – poor thing was probably hit by a car on the dual-carriageway. You need another cat. He's gorgeous.'

He was anything but gorgeous. Greasy-haired with a torn ear, he was malnourished rather than young, but as the vicar set him down on the floor, the cat went straight to the cupboard where I had kept Rhad's food.

'See? He's at home here already.' The vicar was trying to convince me, but I was watching the cat as he sat by the cupboard door, with his head cocked slightly to one side.

He had come back. He was tired, hungry and battered, but it was Rhad all right. His markings were similar to Rhad's. Instead of the tortie beige and black colourings he was mostly white with caramel spots and stripes, but still ultimately the same.

I knew it was Rhad. Which posed a different problem. How could I call him by the name I'd given him? To all intents and purposes, Rhad was gone and this was a stray I was probably going to adopt. But he just stared at me and I swear he smirked as I opened a tin of salmon.

It was Lucy who found out the truth. She came to the house alone the following day and seemed quiet and introspective as I made her a cup of herbal tea.

'Where's Rhad?' she asked, holding the mug in both hands

and sitting down at the kitchen table.

'Like Abby said,' I sat down opposite, wondering where this conversation was going, 'he probably got hit by a car on the dual-carriageway. Poor thing. I think his eyesight was failing.'

'No,' she said. 'Rhad.'

And at that moment, the white and caramel Rhad-Two strolled into the kitchen, jumped up onto the table and sat between us.

'Lucy,' I asked carefully. 'What makes you think this cat might be Rhad? Rhad was tortie.'

'Because he told me.' She hesitated. 'In a dream. Last night.'

'He *spoke* to you? He's a cat, Lucy.'

She shrugged. 'He still spoke to me. He asked me if I ever dreamed about a swing in a huge tree – yes, I *know* it sounds bizarre, Olive, but I swear this is what I dreamed – and he said I had to tell you about it. So here I am, telling you. Like he told me to.'

'He's just a cat.'

She glanced up at me, then. 'He's not just a cat. Any more than you are just a neighbour, Olive. And I do dream. All the time. Abby thinks I'm crazy.' Lucy hesitated. 'I had a red scarf as a child, didn't I? And I lost it on a picnic years ago. Why do I always dream about it? Or is it *just a scarf* too? I'm not a child, anymore, Olive. *Tell me.*'

What was I supposed to do? I had been so careful over the years. I'm still careful now. I try so hard to blend in, to protect Devil's End, to hold this place against those who would do harm. But I couldn't confide in Lucy, no matter how much I might have wanted to; it wouldn't be right – wouldn't be *fair*. I had signed up for this job, but she hadn't, and knowing the dangers would not make her any safer. And she would tell Abby, who would tell her boyfriend, and before you knew it, the whole village would know. At best, I would be ridiculed, and at worst, there would be a modern-day witch-hunt. I didn't need any of it. None of us did.

'How about,' I suggested, 'calling this little thing Rhad? Would that help? Maybe one day you might convince me he is

Rhad-One reincarnated, but I'm not holding my breath.'

She let out a nervous laugh. 'You don't think I'm completely mad, then?'

I held my thumb and first finger a tiny bit apart. 'Maybe just a bit? But who wants to be completely sane? Now finish your tea and leave me in peace. I have work to do this evening.'

Rhad didn't move from the table as I saw Lucy out. As I stood in the kitchen doorway, he jumped down and walked to the back door.

'We're going back, aren't we? To find the scarf.'

Of course we were. That was why he had sent the dream to Lucy. It was her scarf after all and he clearly thought there was a chance his people could get to her through it. I had made the right choice not to tell her.

Back in the barn, the dark recesses behind this year's hay bales were inky-black and forbidding. Rhad jumped up onto the workbench and sat there, idly licking a paw.

'You're not coming?' I thought about it. 'You *can't* come, can you? Not in cat-form, and you can't go home for another seven years anyway.'

Rhad wiped his paw across his torn ear and licked it again, clearly unimpressed with his new body. That first reincarnation was hard for him – over the years he grew into it and each change became easier than the last. I don't think I ever became completely comfortable with the process.

'So what do I do?' I asked. 'You're really not being much help, you know.'

Rhad stared at me.

'How do I get back?'

Nothing.

'Figure it out yourself, Olive. Thanks so much, *cat*.' But I had to do it. I couldn't risk leaving Lucy's scarf to be a chink in my armour, couldn't leave her open to the fey whenever they wanted to get at her – or get at me through her.

Iron. That's what I needed. Rhad had given me a way in and iron would give me an escape. I grabbed a handful of old horseshoe nails from a plant pot and checked to make sure I had a couple of charms in my pouch. Without looking back, I strode towards the back of the barn and into the blackness. I had no way of knowing how long this door of Rhad's would stay open and I suspected it would be seven years before another opportunity arose.

There was none of the dazzling brilliance of last time; this time I was in a clearing in a forest, standing by a rough wooden fence. Except it wasn't a fence at all, was it? Not when I could quite clearly see tiny buds growing on twigs – *branches* – above my head. I put my hand on the bark and felt a faint pulse through my palm.

Not wanting to let go, I trailed my hand across the huge tree trunk and started walking. The pulse grew stronger under my palm and I could hear a faint voice now – soft singing in a strange tongue. It was hypnotic and I wanted to hum along and join in with the song. The tree's pulse resonated with the music and I could feel my own heartbeat slowing to the same rhythm.

And then I saw the child. A girl, with long blonde hair, maybe eight or nine years old and sailing through the air on an old wooden swing. This was what I had seen all those years ago – Lucy and Abby playing together underneath a tree so huge it could be a world in itself.

But the singing came from somewhere else. In the shadow of a tree root stood a woman dressed in shimmering green. I'd seen her before too, wearing Lucy's scarf. A wood nymph, maybe? If this truly was the world tree, then its spirit might be a formidable enemy. And I didn't need any more enemies.

The swoosh of the swing was in time with the pulse of the tree, the rhythm of the song and the beat of my heart. Everything in perfect harmony, staged almost, as if they were waiting for my arrival.

Perhaps they were.

The woman stopped singing; the rhythm broke and suddenly everything was out of step. A note of dissonance. The swing slowed, branches creaking high above. The pulse died away and my heart rate increased.

'You are welcome,' the tree sprit said.

I didn't feel welcome. I felt like an intruder – the stranger in a strange land. Last time, my apple thief had saved me, but this time I was on my own.

'You have something that belongs to me,' I said. 'I'd like it back, please.'

She laughed, a discord of musical notes. It wasn't malevolent – just ambivalent. Capricious, maybe. 'Greetings, Lady Olive. But I fear there is nothing of yours here.'

'The scarf?'

'The scarf? Oh, you mean this bauble?' Out of nowhere she produced Lucy's scarf, like a magician conjuring a white dove. She pulled it through her fingers, the silk sliding across smooth pale skin. 'This is not yours to ask for.'

'And yet ask for it I must.' It was hard not to talk like them. So formal and contrived. Words could be weapons here.

'Then you must give me something in return. A bargain!' She laughed again, winding the scarf around her neck. 'Something personal, perhaps?'

What? I had nothing on me, apart from the nails and I doubted iron would be her gift of choice. I could snatch the scarf and maybe fight my way home, but I would still be in debt and the fey always honour – and collect – their debts. To be free of them, I would have to wipe the slate clean.

'What would you want from me?' I asked carefully, watching the child from the corner of my eye. Was this another human child, or simple trickery to lure me into a trap?

The woman lifted the end of the scarf to her nose and inhaled deeply. 'Ah, the smell of innocence. Children are such precious creatures, don't you think?' She pursed her lips. 'I require … a memory.'

'A memory?' I didn't understand.

'A memory. One of my choosing. Human memories are so much more *vibrant* than my own; so fleeting and mortal. So *alive*. I should love to have one for myself.'

It seemed a silly price to pay. Just a memory. Presumably I wouldn't even notice since I wouldn't remember it. 'What kind of memory?' I asked.

'Something important to you. The more emotion, the more succulent the memory. But do not worry,' she added, 'I would not take your identity from you, nor the memory of where you live or how to breathe. That would not be proper. But I am lonely and would ask for a memory to comfort me.'

'All right.' I had no choice, really. Not if I wanted to protect Lucy. It might be another seven years before Rhad could engineer another opportunity.

'Then you must close your eyes.' She was more serious now. 'It will not hurt.'

I did as she instructed and found my thoughts drifting beyond my control, as if somebody was flipping through the pages of my life. Thoughts of my childhood, of my parents, of my twin sister Poppy, of the night before she disappeared when we were just seventeen – the night when I knew our lives would change forever … no! Not that memory! Not that one.

A fair exchange. More musical laughter and something soft in my hands. I opened my eyes and saw Lucy's scarf. The swing, the child and the tree-spirit were gone and I was alone and wondering what I had done.

For a moment, I had an overwhelming urge to sit down with my back against this ancient tree and just give up. Why did everything have to be so hard? But I had to protect Lucy and Devil's End, and in the end it had cost me … what? I wasn't even sure anymore. I couldn't remember. Now I just needed to get home.

I took an iron nail from my pocket and pressed it into the tree with my thumb. The tree sighed and the air shivered. I did it again and again, until I had used all the nails, not caring that the tree was screaming and I was maybe damaging something irreplaceable. I was only human, after all. Human and hurting, weighed down by responsibility.

The world began to pull away from me. I felt like I was standing on an island and all about me were shifting sands, unreality, uncertainty spinning into blackness. Nothing. No direction and I was scared to take a step, not knowing which way to go. And then I saw a light ahead. I focussed on it, gave it all my attention and willed it closer. I'm not sure whether I approached the source, or it came closer to me, but as the darkness around me brightened, I saw a small white and caramel cat.

Every seven years or so, you changed, didn't you, Rhad? Sometimes black, sometimes tabby, sometimes ginger, you came back to me in so many ways. And this morning you are missing again. Maybe this will be the time you *don't* come back, when your sentence is completed, your exile over. Rhadamanthus. Apple thief. Friend. I wonder what will become of you when I'm gone?

THE POPPET
Jan Edwards

There is a lifetime of clutter in this cottage of mine. Several lifetimes in point of fact, and we Hawthorne women, as Lobelia had reminded me, are merely guardians; though we all make our individual marks in passing.

Take that oak dresser for instance. It belonged to my grandmother, Hester. The sea chest beneath the window came from Dulcin, who had tenure before her. And this grimoire? A gypsy woman Lobelia brought it to me, though it first belonged to Dulcin's mother. I have a great many books of reference on my shelves. I am told some of them are quite rare and valuable. But this battered thing is the repository of the Hawthorne legacy and the most precious to me. I've tried to ensure that I added my share of wisdom and caveat over the years. A record of all the important events and findings, and yes, the warnings used to advise our future generations.

I have been clearing the decks, ready for my successor, and stumbled across this little doll – a poppet. It doesn't look very much, but it is the final remnant of one of the most dangerous events to happen, even here in Devil's End – with the exception of that incident with the Doctor, naturally, but that was a couple of years later! This doll has lain in the attic, locked inside a lacquered tea caddy for a very long time. Nothing magical about the box itself except that it is lead-lined. Useless in a modern age because we've realised what lead does to the body, but that toxic metal made it perfect for keeping such a monstrosity under control. I got the idea from the Brigadier. He said that if lead could keep nuclear waste under control it should be effective against emanations of any kind, whatever their source of power.

So what could this doll have that makes it so dangerous? It's quite a pretty thing in a quaint fashion, and the very image of Josephine Bingley, or Josephine Winstanley as she became. Say what you will about Melissa Fenn she was a gifted craftswoman. That lumpen seam clawing its way up the doll's back is my work and lacks any hint of finesse. I have many skills and interests but needlecraft has never been one of them.

See that photo over there on the wall of Josephine's wedding? The entire village was there and seeing them all smiles and posh frocks it's hard to believe that just twenty-four hours earlier they had come so close to losing that radiant bride forever. And all down to Melissa Fenn's abominable fetishes.

I would have destroyed this last poppet a long time ago had I not feared for Josephine. She's been gone for a long time so it hardly matters now but holding the thing still gives me the willies. When I first picked it out of the caddy an hour ago I felt a small shock wave run through my fingers right up to my elbow, as if I had grabbed a battery with wet hands. It has an unnatural warmth, which cannot be wholly attributed to being so close to the fire. I can't help feeling Melissa Fenn's spirit has somehow awoken at my touch. Or Goddess forbid some vestige of poor Josephine?

Those beautifully sewn eyes are fixed on me and a cold slither of remembered fear is running down my spine. Josie had been like a sister all the time we were growing up. Not as close as I was with Poppy of course, but as close as girls can be without being related by blood. That was until Melissa Fenn came to Devil's End and begun to exert her power over others.

Poppets are a powerful tool and never more dangerous than when they look so very appealing. That was the simplicity of the Fenn woman's methodology; having people clamouring to buy the very object of their doom.

Dulcin Hawthorne referred to them as mommets. To the ancient Greeks they were kolossoi. I myself have always known them as poppets, though I realise most think they are Voodoo dolls because of films and television. Whatever the label witches and shamans everywhere have used them in some form.

I have a particular distaste for them because of this very thing here in my hand, fashioned in the image of my oldest friend. It is a dangerous piece of mischief and I would have destroyed it a long time ago, had I not feared that a little piece of Josephine remained inside it. But I digress. Perhaps I should go back to the beginning to enable you to understand that.

Melissa Fenn arrived in Devil's End in the summer of 1969 to open a hair salon and beauty parlour and we, the village that is, thought her a little cosmopolitan for a rural backwater such as Devil's End. There was no denying she was good at what she did and she threw herself into village life right from the start. Her enthusiasm and what appeared to be acts of genuine kindness made her popular so that people soon forgot she was an incomer. She offered haircuts at reduced rates for the elderly and donated tokens for beauty therapies as raffle prizes at the summer fete. Everybody thought she was simply wonderful, myself included.

Her salon had become quite the institution by the time she began making her little facsimiles of local worthies. They were all terribly amusing at first. Harmless fun at the expense of friends and neighbours, or more often themselves, and it was uncanny how each one captured the character of its owner. It wasn't long before almost everyone in the village had their own little *doppelgänger*. My knowledge of such things had made me wary but it was Rhadamanthus who started me thinking that there was something genuinely amiss.

Rhad possessed an uncanny sense for all things magical which came in very useful on any number of occasions. Never more so than with the 'fabulous' Miss Fenn.

It was one of those cold, bright days that begged for one to get out for some fresh air and exercise. I was rooting around in the border behind the hedge, clearing out the dead stems and suchlike, as one does in the winter months and Rhadamanthus was 'supervising' my efforts from the path in his usual fashion, when Melissa Fenn came by.

She was clutching one of her dolls in front of her, like a wedding bouquet, though I barely noticed the doll itself. Not at first. It was Ms Fenn who had my attention because she looked so very odd. She was not so much walking as progressing down the centre of the lane, head high and stepping slowly and deliberately. The only time I've ever seen anybody move quite like that was the time when the Bishop came to bless the new lectern: pomp and ceremony has never been to my liking.

Ms Fenn's lips were moving and I caught fragments, a few words and phrases, but nothing that made immediate sense. Yet it was familiar in a way that chilled me far more than the winter air, and beyond her whisperings there was nothing else to be heard, not so much as a single bird fluting from the hedgerow, a fact that didn't register with me until later. I could not bring myself to call out, though I wanted to. I could only watch as she grew closer.

Rhadamanthus was not taken in by Miss Fen's utterings. He took one look, arched his back, and hissed. I've never known him do that to anyone before. He might stalk away with tail and nose held high but that is the limit of his disregard. Yet there he was, backing away, with spine arched and tail standing out like a bottle-brush, screeching like a proverbial banshee.

The Fenn woman stopped dead in her tracks and turned slowly, like a reptile, to glare at poor Rhad. He was crouched low now, still hissing like a mad thing of course, his right paw raised, boxing the air between them in sharp jabs.

I am not sure who was more surprised when the wretched woman hissed back. This was not the kind of pretend yowl people use when a cat talks to them, but a virulent and venomous hiss that came from the depths of her chest. Rhadamanthus's ears flattened further and for a long moment they glowered at each other, before Rhad turned and fled past where I was kneeling. As he did so, without breaking his stride, he took a swipe at me, slicing three parallel bloody tracks across the back of my wrist.

I was jolted out of my curious stasis. I hauled myself to my feet, and from the look on her face I honestly thought Miss Fenn was going to attack me. Perhaps she would have, had the postman not been walking up from Vicarage Way.

Instead of physical violence she tucked her chin down and glowered at me from under her fringe. The amulet around my neck, the one Poppy had left behind on the night she vanished, felt heavy and cold against my skin in warning. My hand went to it by habit and we stared at each other. One hears of rabbits being mesmerised by headlights and I can empathise with the poor creatures because I was quite unable to do anything sensible.

The Fenn woman was muttering once more, but fell silent when the postie called out 'Good afternoon' as he passed.

My limbs were suddenly my own again. I stepped back several paces and held the amulet toward her. Whether it was the ancient charm or distance that broke her hold I don't know, but broken it was. Miss Fenn gave me one final look of pure hatred and stalked away.

The incident was alarming to say the least and I hurried indoors to consult my books. At that time I could find nothing in them to explain what had occurred, nor what might have caused Rhad's aberrant behaviour. Rhadamanthus himself vanished for several days after the episode. I have no idea where he goes to, though I have my suspicions, but he was not normally one to desert me in times of peril. As nothing further occurred for almost a week I had to believe that my physical reaction to Ms Fenn had come from both the shock of Rhad's attack and standing too quickly.

That week's lull ended when I went into the Post Office for a strip of stamps. The moment I opened the door I knew something was amiss. I was greeted by that awkward, shuffling silence, which occurs when you are that 'someone under discussion' who has arrived unexpectedly.

The gathering parted, leaving me free to approach the counter without needing to queue, which was an oddity in itself. The etiquette of queuing is inviolate and those permitted to jump to the head was usually confined to expectant mothers and the very old, and I was neither. 'Good morning, Mrs Taylor.

Chilly day isn't it.'

'It is.'

I waited for more, but all the Postmistress had to offer was a stony glare, whilst the gossips gathered at the other end of the counter, pretending to be interested in the racks of greetings cards, avoided eye contact.

'I'd like six second class stamps, please, Mrs Taylor.'

She tore a strip of the gummed rectangles from a sheet and slid them under the grille slot with a curt, 'Three shillings,' and bristled in silence as I counted out the coins. I could feel the surreptitious attention of everyone there upon me, and not a word uttered amongst them. I had no idea why I was being treated that way, but the ceiling didn't have to fall for me to realise it was not the best place to be. I picked up my stamps with a cheery 'thank you,' and beat a retreat.

Hurrying across the street I saw Annie Botting emerging from the rectory, where she cleans three mornings a week. Now Annie had been in the previous week asking for a herbal salve for her dog and because I'd been drying a fresh batch of herbs I had asked her to call back. It was out of character for her not to return.

'Annie. I was hoping to see you.' I waved to her and began to cross the road.

She plainly heard me call because she paused and half turned in my direction. But at the moment she spotted me she ducked her head down and put on an extraordinary turn of speed for a woman of her age.

'I have that ointment for Rufus …'

I was astonished when the woman turned sharp left and scuttled away down Lid Lane without a backward glance. She was going in the opposite direction to her house and also the opposite way to myself – a point that did not elude me.

The Post Office door bell jangled behind me and I spun around to see two of Mrs Taylor's gossip-group lurking in the porch, watching me stand there in the middle of the road like a lost sheep. When I took a step toward them both scuttled away like frightened mice, leaving me alone in a totally deserted street.

I hurried back to the cottage, puzzled and frankly upset by those two incidents. My feelings turned to frustration, and also a certain amount of anger, as the example set by those women developed into a pattern over the following days. Folks I had known all my life were doing their utmost to avoid me and absolutely nobody was visiting the cottage. Not even the lovelorn and lonely seeking charms and love potions. Yet Melissa Fenn, the newcomer, was being fêted like some conquering hero.

Oh, I realise it sounds so petty when I put it that way but it had become so very obvious that I was not just being ignored. I was being actively 'shunned'. I was positive that had nothing to do with anything I had done to the good people of Devil's End, or not directly at least, yet I'd become the stranger in my own land. The only explanation was that, due to my being unaffected by Melissa Fenn, she was seeking to cut me from the herd.

It would be nice to be able to say that this was the first occasion that external forces have effectively put me on the outside, but it wasn't, nor was it the last. It is on these occasions that the Hawthorne legacy comes into its own. Before she left me, Lobelia had instilled in me the absolute imperative of placing protections around the cottage at regular intervals; especially in a place like Devil's End. This is not a selfish act but a sensible precaution. Or, as the Brigadier would have said, securing operational bases as an essential part of your campaign and I had no doubt by that time that there was a substantial darkness in our midst that required me to go into battle.

Once the wards around my home had been replenished I moved on to the cavern beneath St Michael's church, because that is the seat of the forces that draw evil creatures such as Melissa Fenn to us. I considered including the ancient mound, the Devil's Hump, up on the Goat's Back ridge beyond the village but decided not to stretch myself too thin and hurried home to search out fresh auguries in the runes.

Reading the runes is as much a part of me as breathing and

the set that I use has been passed down through many generations of guardians; blue-stone pebbles with the sigils carved into them, filled with beaten copper. That evening I barely noticed their beauty as I cast once, twice, three times and saw nothing at all; merely the blank tile accompanied by nothing that made any sense. It was as if a thick blanket had been thrown over the entire cottage. Something new and disturbing for me and I pushed rising panic firmly back where it belonged and unveiled my crystal ball. The one thing 'gazing' required was a cool head. Taking a few deep breaths I gazed long and hard into the murky quartz globe but try as I may there was nothing to see beyond boiling mists. I replaced the cloth with a sigh, sitting back in my chair feeling exhausted, and not a little frightened, that all of my divination skills should have deserted me in the same day. Something was very much wrong in Devil's End, but without my usual sources to lean on to gauge what and how there was nothing to be done but wait.

It was yet another week later that I found myself reading the runes for much happier circumstances when I was visited by Josephine Bingley. I was thrilled to see her, not only as my closest friend but also because she was my first visitor in several days.

'What are you looking for?' I asked. 'The wedding is this weekend. A little late to be asking if Cedric is your Mr Right.'

She grinned, a little embarrassed I think. 'I don't really know. Cedric is a funny old stick, and I know people think he's too old for me, but I do love him.' She shrugged. 'Wedding jitters I suppose.' There was a hint of uncertainty in her tone. 'Jitters,' she said again. 'Or perhaps not.'

She looked so very sad. I reached out to take her hand, and tried not to notice how she flinched at my touch. 'Is everything alright between you and Cedric?' I asked.

'Yes … of course. Why would you ask?'

Again, that fractional uncertainty. I gained the impression she was less unsure of her answer so much as confused by the question. 'Well let's see what the runes have to tell us.' I held the bag out and Josephine took it, not bothering to shake it, just delved her right hand straight in to retrieve three stones.

She held them in her clenched fist, with eyes closed, concentrating on the outcome, and I didn't have the heart to remind her the time for influencing the draw was whilst her hand was still in the bag. After a few long seconds she let the pebbles drop onto the cloth and stared at them before looking hopefully toward me.

And I – Goddess help me, there isn't a day goes by when I don't regret my reply to that reading – I broke my own unwritten rules and gave her the answers I thought she wanted to hear; which were very far removed from what I saw.

Kenaz the Beacon, reversed, which stands for withdrawal and loss; Berkhana the Goddess, reversed, that is unwanted change; Hagalaz, the force of destruction. For a bride looking for good things to herald her wedding it would be hard to get anything less encouraging. Unlike Tarot there is no 'death' rune as such but this was as close as could be got.

I have always made it a rule to be truthful with my advice, but, at the same time never to reveal darker readings because the power of suggestion is all too real. Josephine Bingley and I were always close. I was every bit the sister she never had as she was to me, and who was I to destroy her dreams? I never saw Cedric Winstanley as the ideal man for Josephine it was true. He was much older for one thing. For Josie that was not the issue and obviously her opinion was the only one that held any weight. So far as she was concerned he knew horses, which was how they came to meet, and they adored each other, so when she told me they were getting married? I was happy for her.

Since Miss Fenn arrived our friendship had become a little cool and that had truly puzzled me. We had been friends for so long that it hurt to know she took the word of a stranger against mine. When I looked at those runes, those copper shapes glowing in the light, I began to understand. I could not tell her what I saw there. Not just because of the risk that I might influence her without cause, but, selfishly, because I knew that it could end our friendship forever. So I took a deep breath and

I lied through my back teeth.

'All good,' I said. 'Yours will be a long and happy marriage.'

'Is that all they say?'

Her tone held an edge. Did she realise I was fibbing? I'd been reading for her for so many years and it would be naive of me to think she had not picked up some knowledge of them in that time. I scooped the stones back into their bag before she could memorise them; feeling the thunk of each one like the tolling of a bell. A sound that was echoed by the chiming of my mantle clock.

'Goodness, its five o'clock already.' She smiled at me and touched my arm. 'Final wedding rehearsal is at six-thirty. You won't forget now will you, Olly?'

'Wild horses, my dear. Fire breathing dragons. Nothing will keep me away, I promise you.'

Josephine laughed that loud, hearty laugh of hers as she shrugged on her coat and crammed a knitted hat firmly over her ears. 'I shall see you later then. Don't forget. 6.30pm, sharp.' And then she was gone.

At the appointed time I fed the recently-returned Rhad his evening bowl of fish and slowly dressed myself against the elements. It would not have taken much to dissuade me, at that moment, to stay at home. I told myself it was because of the weather but the thought of standing in that church amongst all of those people filled me with dread.

As I crossed the darkened green the first few flakes of snow were already jigging around me on a rising wind. The church doors basking in a circle of light from a single lamp over the porch was welcoming despite my misgivings.

Opening and closing the studded oak doors of St Michael's Church, with their massive cast-iron latch, was impossible to accomplish in silence. The rattle and clunk echoed all through the building, right up to the chancel steps where Josephine and her wedding party stood. I had only seen her a few hours before and I was appalled at the changes in her. That healthy aura of glowing blues and greens had turned dark, muddy red that radiated toxic, anger.

My certainty that something was very wrong increased when Josephine turned in my direction to look me up and down, her features pulled downwards in disapproval. 'What do you want? Witch.'

Her words rose upward and roiled through the rafters with a chilling clarity on that final word. I was completely and utterly devastated. 'The rehearsal of course,' I said. 'You told me 6.30pm sharp, and here I am.'

'And now you can go again.'

'But … I don't understand. I'm your bridesmaid. I need to know what I am supposed to be doing tomorrow. Can't have me tripping over your train or dropping the bouquet, can we.'

'No, we can't. Which is why I've decided to have Melissa as my bridesmaid.'

'But you asked me.' I don't think I was screaming, not aloud, though my throat ached with those words.

Josephine glared the length of the nave, her hands on her hips. 'Did I? I really don't recall that. Why would I ask you? An old maid? Because that's what you are. And what you will always be. Now go home.'

Stunned did not begin to describe the pain her words sent through me. She 'said' she had forgotten. Forgotten? I knew she had to be in the grip of some malevolent geas. 'What have I done to offend you? Whatever it is I apologise. You know I wouldn't hurt you for the world.'

'Since you ask?' She marched down the nave and reached out to grab at the ankh and missed. 'I don't know how you have the nerve to wear that in here.' I dodged back as she tried to snatch it again. 'Witch,' she said. 'You … are a witch. And I don't know how you have the nerve to set foot in here.'

I clasped my talisman tightly in my right hand. 'The Vicar has certainly never objected.'

'Well I am objecting now,' she replied. 'I don't want you as my bridesmaid. How can I have someone like you traipsing down the aisle behind me? I've asked Melissa and that is all you need to know.'

I was simply devastated. My oldest and dearest friend was

forsaking me for somebody she barely knew. 'But Josie …' I stared her straight in the eye, searching for some reason for this change of heart.

It was Josephine who looked away first. 'Well? What are you waiting for? Melissa is to be my flower girl and that is the end of it. Now go away!'

The rest of the gathering shuffled nervously. I stood my ground, looking around me for my usurper, who was conspicuously absent. 'If that is your choice then I shall have to accept that. But where is she?'

'Oh … she's been held up, but she'll be here. Now stop blithering.' Josephine smiled slyly. 'You do know everyone here calls you the "mad woman"? All your stupid runes and tripping around the woods. Just go back to that brute of a cat. He's the only male you will ever have in your life. Now if you don't mind, the Vicar was about to show me where we shall sign the register.'

I could hardly believe what I was hearing. Everyone knew I was a witch. Yet despite that they all came to me, to consult the runes and for remedies, or the odd love philtre. Of all people in our community who would not give a damn about my background and beliefs it should have been my childhood friend standing across the aisle from me. We stared at each other in a silence that stretched far beyond the wooden pews and stone walls surrounding us.

It was the eyes that gave her away. Their warmth, which had been her abiding gift, was missing, and in their place a stagnant chill, devoid of all human emotion. I knew with crushing certainty that whomever it was standing opposite me in that church it was not Josephine Bingley: that dear kind girl I had known all my life. It couldn't be. She would never talk to me this way.

Something needed to be done and the solution was not going to involve a few herbs and nice words. People refer to me as a white witch, which is a misleading term, but I seldom correct people who use it. Far simpler to allow them the comfort that it brings in knowing they are dealing with a kindly creature. The truth is a witch is a witch, be they white witches or not. Like most I adhere to the creed 'and it harm none', and I like to think I err on the lighter side … but I know what the dark side involves, having stepped over that invisible line several times when there was no other option. The power that I sensed from the woman glaring back at me, however, was not some minor hex or binding but a far grimmer prospect.

There was a genuine malevolence there before me now. I could not fail to recognise forces raised by unknown incantations emanating from her as an unseen yet tangible aura. Thick and ugly. Coiling around her like the tentacles of some monster from the deep, though we are a long way from the sea. It was darkening her aura to the deep sickly red of stagnating anger, which rocked me back as a physical blow. This was no ordinary spell of deception. The flesh and blood of my oldest friend no longer contained her true essence and there was no doubt in my mind. She was possessed.

I watched her retreat toward the vestry and stood there like a dummy as the doors closed behind them. I was all alone. I closed my eyes briefly and gathered my senses around me before making my way back along the nave, past the screens, and through to the vestibule. My hand was on the round iron handle and I was about to plunge back into the night when I felt a draught from another direction. The door to the left of the vestibule was slightly ajar. I paused. That door was always locked, unless the bell tower was in use, ever since young Jimmy Brewer had gone up alone on a dare and slipped at the very top of the spiral steps, breaking both of his arms and fracturing his skull.

A glance back toward the chancel showed nobody watching, so I slipped through the half open door – and almost fell over Melissa Fenn seated on a wooden chair at the foot of the staircase.

I began to apologise out of habit, as one does when one bumps into somebody, regardless of who is at fault. When I recognised her I steeled myself for some pithy comment that I was sure would arise, but none came. She remained absolutely still with both eyes wide open and her lips curved into a faint smile. Though she was seated she held that ghastly Poppet clutched tightly before her in both hands in a pose eerily like that which she had adopted on the day Rhad had taken it upon himself to hiss and spit.

The hairs on my neck prickled.

'Miss Fenn?' I said. 'I'm sorry – are you unwell? Melissa?' I waved my hand in front of her face. Not a flicker of response. Not that I was expecting one because she was clearly locked into some fugue state, but it is always worth checking. I reached out and felt her wrist for a pulse. It was there, though achingly slow and thready.

I hadn't a great deal of first-hand experience with poppets before then but I sensed an unmistakable taint of the arcane and stepped back to examine her from a safer distance. Darkness writhed around Miss Fenn's inert form like a silver-grey shimmer. I was thoroughly revolted – and just a little relieved because I knew what I had to do. That thing in her hands had to be destroyed.

My fingers closed reluctantly around the cloth body to tug it free of her fingers. It pulsed and twitched in my grasp and I almost dropped it in surprise, shock even, except there was no sense of evil around the poppet itself as I'd expected. Only fear and sadness and pleading … and quite unlike Melissa Fenn in any shape or form.

Raised voices from the vestry warned me that I would not be alone for much longer, and the tasks uppermost in my mind were to separate the Fenn woman from that poppet, and to prevent her from completing whatever invocation she had begun. I gave the doll a last yank that pried it free. Ramming the doll into my bag I slipped away into the night. The priority now was to reach the safety of the cottage and consult my grimoire.

I spent a long while scouring not only the pages of my grimoire but as many tomes in my library as I thought might help, and all of them told me the same thing. That poppets containing the hair or nail clippings of a victim have huge power over them and how destroying the poppet without the exact incantation used in the effigies manufacture can occasionally result in dire effects.

I had no doubt that the poppet contained clippings of Josephine's hair. It certainly explained her bizarre behaviour in the church. Like almost every adult in the village, including most of my coven, she had visited Melissa Fenn's salon. I myself was immune because I have always been careful to burn any nail or hair clippings of my own. That I had never needed to go into the salon meant I had no way of knowing who could be trusted.

Perhaps that was fitting? Devil's End had been under my family's protection for centuries and as the incumbent Hawthorne it was down to me to see that Melissa Fenn's influence was removed.

I stared at the grimoire, pondering my next move. There was no way of knowing exactly how long I had to find an answer. No more than a few hours, certainly. Once Melissa Fenn realised the poppet had been taken she would be sure to eliminate the culprit.

'And unlike myself,' I said to Rhadamanthus who was curled as close to the hearth as he could get, 'Our Miss Fenn has the advantage of knowing exactly who was on what I was sure will be a very short list of suspects. Provided she ever climbed out of her trance.'

I had drawn the conclusion that finding her in that state was that her control of so many people at once required all of her concentration. A case of massed astral projection? It seemed unlikely and why from the church? Had I been inclined to such acts I would have done it from a far safer spot. Lobelia's mantra of protection was far too deeply ingrained to be so rash.

I flipped open the grimoire and began turning leaves at random, eyes closed, allowing my mind to go blank and select the answer by divination. My fingers stopped their riffling and I stared at the page on display. Not making generic poppets, or at least not directly, nor astral projection.

'Of course. How can I be so stupid? This entire charade is

about replacing Josephine as Cedric's bride.' Rhad glared at me through slitted eyes and then yawned, curling his rough, pink tongue between twin sets of pointed canines. His mouth opened so wide you could barely see there was a head attached to it. It was a yawn that plainly said he could not be bothered with an idiot such as myself and that he was in no mood to assist.

'Think about it, Rhadamanthus,' I told him. 'Squire Cedric employs and houses most of Devil's End, from the Vicar downwards. He's also the local Magistrate. Landlord to almost everyone for miles around. In short? Whoever is the wife to the Squire of Devil's End will be mistress of us all. Poor Cedric. He's a bit of a blockhead but even if it were not Josephine at risk I still wouldn't wish him bound to a mistress of the black arts.'

We stared at the fire, listening to the crack and tink of embers shifting and settling, lost in our own thoughts. It was I who broke the tableau, throwing more logs onto the fire and pouring more tea from the pot sitting on the hearth before bending over the pages to read and memorise as much information as I could.

The ceremony was simple enough, though obviously fraught with danger. So many things to go wrong but my choices were few and time was of the essence.

Setting the book on the low table at my side I took the poppet and carefully slit it open to locate the phylactery, which is the shamanic pouch sewn into the body that holds the doll's power. I parted the layers of padding and slid the leather pad out for closer inspection. It felt warm in my hand and a quiet yet clearly discernible tapping pattered against my fingers. I knew, beyond any shadow of doubt, that this was Josephine. I was literally holding the essence of my oldest friend in the palm of my hand. Her body might well be strutting around the church planning the wedding ceremony for the next day, but the part of Josie that mattered was there in that gris-gris. Which in turn could only mean a portion of Melissa Fenn had already taken up residence within her intended host.

It seems I had been closer than I thought with astral projection but so wrong on scale. Fenn had left her body in the tower stairwell to inhabit just one body – my friend, Josephine. Yet there were also scores, perhaps even hundreds of these poppets around the village, each one of which needed to be under her control for her plan to succeed. My own pulse was racing as I read the final paragraph's dire warning. *Should you fail to return each aura to its rightful place before the sunrise there is grave risk that said switch might be permanent.*

'This is not good, Rhadamanthus,' I muttered. 'All Mellissa Fenn needs to do is allow her old shell to "die", and she will now that to all intents and purposes she has become Josephine Bingley. Once she goes on to become Josephine Winstanley, she'll be mistress of this entire village, with access to the powers beneath St Michael's cavern and the barrow beyond the village, and that does not bear thinking about for the whole country.'

Rhadamanthus regarded me through sleepy eyes and began to rub his chin against the leather corners of the book, uttering urgent chirruping sounds.

'Yes, I know, keep reading. Now what do I need to reverse this cursed spell?'

It took me less than ten minutes to gather all but one of the things I would need in my bag. The final ingredient was the most crucial and the hardest of all to obtain. Without it, with all the best will and all the power-raising in the world, I would fail, but I could not afford to dwell on that outcome. I'd undertaken several major interventions since I had taken up my role as the guardian of Devil's End, but this was the first occasion that I had acted totally alone. I will admit to feeling more than a little apprehensive and wondered if perhaps this coming ritual was beyond me.

Lobelia's voice echoed down the years, telling me to grow a backbone. Rhadamanthus sat up and yowled at me, as though he had heard her also. Perhaps he had, one never knows with that cat. It was the push that I needed. A few deep invigorating breaths … and I plunged straight back into the night.

The snow had begun falling in earnest while I had been studying the texts. It lay thickly against the hedges and verges, and was whipping past me now on a wind in as close to a blizzard as we get in these parts. I had quite a struggle, leaning into that bitter gale, to reach the Church and I was minded to believe the Elements themselves were attempting to keep me from my task. Fortunately elementals were always my speciality. A few words and I quieted them enough to enter the church without drawing attention to myself.

I eased the door open and slipped inside, closing the latch slowly, as though made of spider's silk, to make as little sound as possible. Once the solid oak door was closed, and the howling wind was no more than muffled whimpers, I crept to the inner door and listened for any hint of whomever shared the space with me.

It was absurdly quiet after the pandemonium in progress when I had left, though logically, I realised, most of the gathering would have long since fled for home. The first thing I looked for was the inert figure of Melissa Fenn, but she was no longer seated in the vestibule where I had left her. I toyed with the idea that the Fenn woman might have abandoned her plan and re-inhabited her own form – only a passing fancy because her sort would never capitulate so easily.

The second thing was that there was no electric light, though as power cuts in such weather conditions were normal in these parts I was not surprised by that. Peering out into the chancel I noted candles burning on the altar and from the flickering shadows I concluded there had to be several spaced along the Nave. As the Vicar was hardly going to leave naked flames unattended someone had to be in there with me, and the list of potential suspects was an exceptionally short one.

I sidled along the western side-aisle toward the pulpit and peered along each pew in turn. Finally I found her. A solitary figure kneeling on a cassock two rows from the altar, as if in prayer, motionless and silent. Melissa Fenn. I drew back into the shadow and considered my best course of action. This *had* to be a trap. The Fenn woman had moved out into an open area where approach could not be carried out unseen. She knew I would be coming back and all she needed do was wait.

The wind was up again, whistling through every crack in

brick and window, rattling the doors as if the elementals themselves were demanding violent entry. Impatient, impertinent even. Time was running out.

I crept forward, glad that my choice of footwear was sturdy brogues that could move across stone flags in relative silence when required. Heel-toe … heel-toe, closer by feet and yards until I was almost within touching distance of the motionless figure.

Melissa Fenn remained fixed, like some poseable doll waiting for its owner to play once more. The similarity came to me quite forcibly when I noted how her empty hands were raised not in prayer as I had supposed but slightly apart, her fingers crooked, as though holding the memory of the poppet that had been plucked from her. It made my next task much easier. Or so I hoped.

I slid the final yard along the pew behind her; reached into my pocket, fumbled for scissors, leaned forward and snipped a lock of hair from the back of her head.

As the blades sheared together and severed a hank of silky strands, ancient stone around us began to quiver, showering us both with dust. Lights, suspended from beams over our heads, swayed and flickered. The noise rose, and I could swear there were voices in that howling, a violent screeching without words.

Hymn books scattered in the air, floating around my head, before plummeting down to the stone flags with heavy thunks. The whole building had begun to shake and larger pieces of detritus fell into the aisle and over dark oaken benches. And still the Fenn woman sat, staring vacantly ahead of her.

A carved stone head set high up in the transept crashed onto the pew in front of us and I threw my arm up to shield my face. I wondered briefly if I would be able to save the both of us, because it went against my instinct to allow her to die. Another ragged ball of masonry struck the edge of the pulpit, shattering the elaborately carved lectern and balustrade. I shielded my head from slivers of flying wood debris: I ran.

My breath was whisked away on an unnatural wind the

moment I set foot outside of the building, and I could barely stand up against it. Nor could I see through the blizzard that was whipped up. Staying where I was could not be an option and I launched myself into the storm to lurch from one grave marker to the next for several yards. Finally I sought refuge in the lee of one of the larger tombs and strained to catch sight of anything or anyone in pursuit.

If Fenn had left the church had she lost my trail already?

Above the wind I heard noises resonating from within the walls. Why hadn't she followed me? I could only imagine she had a counter spell and assumed I would make for the cottage giving her time to thwart me at a distance. She had not allowed that going even a short distance had exhausted me, however, and time was the commodity in shortest supply. With luck it would never occur to her that I would be rash enough to finish the ritual right there in the teeth of the storm. Crouching down, using my own slender bulk as a shield, I cleared a space in the snow and emptied out my bag of supplies.

The spells I was about to embark on were the hardest I had ever attempted and my fingers tingled with anticipation and fear. They were also numbing rapidly with cold and I was glad I'd had the foresight to thread needles before I'd left the cottage; one with black wool and the other crimson silk. I used the latter to stitch Miss Fenn's hair into a fresh phylactery, and crammed it into the doll. As I said before, I am no seamstress, and it is hard to sew in a howling gale and without light.

Now came the final phase. I began to mutter the words of the binding that I had committed to memory. Before I had finished the third pass the noises from the church increased, enraged howlings that could have frozen me where I crouched had the temperature in the churchyard been any warmer. That foul entity inhabiting Josephine's body had became instantly aware of me – and of my counter magic. Hampered by her distance from her true form I had a little time still.

I sewed and I chanted, and marked each pass of the incantation with a French knot stitch. Yes, I realise the grimoire specified a Chinese form, but time was not standing still and I had to trust that the substitution made no appreciable difference.

> Portals be still, at one with my mind,
> I hold thee fast, to make and to bind,
> Close you now, be sealed by my knot,
> Your being be bound, 'til time has forgot.
> So may it be in three times three.

I chanted on, head stooped and shoulders tensed, trying my best to ignore the very real prospect of violent interruption and death. I barely had the ninth and final stitch fastened when Mellissa Fenn burst through the church door – fully in control of her own body and bent on stopping me before my counter-invocation could sever all links with poor Josephine.

I stumbled to my feet, staggering as the full force of the wind hit me and the Fenn creature hurled herself toward me. She seemed almost to be flying, her arms outstretched with hands held as rigid claws, her face contorted into a demon rictus.

Instinctively I raised the doll to face her, and bellowed my binding for all I was worth across the space between us. Time slowed to a crawl. My elementals of wind and precipitation screamed in chorus, drowning out her words of counter spell.

The bells tolled their basso support … louder … and louder … and louder.

And then?

It was done.

I don't know what happened at the very end. That probably sounds rather lame but it's the truth. I must have staggered home and fallen exhausted into my chair because that was where I woke a few hours later.

It was the dawn sun peeping through the windows that roused me. I hauled myself to my feet feeling as if I had been beaten with sticks over every part of my body, and went to the window that overlooked the green. The church stood proudly on the far side. Intact and innocent and clad in its fresh mantle of virginal white, it gave off that air of Christmas card perfection. Time slipped past and that pristine snow had begun to glow such a beautiful, delicate shade of pink of a new day. Everything fresh and bright – as any wedding day should be.

I often wonder what happened to Melissa Fenn. No body was ever found and the mystery of her disappearance was never spoken of. Perhaps people remembered their actions and were ashamed of them, or more likely once free of the woman's influence they simply didn't remember. It doesn't matter all that much.

Within a day people were calling at the cottage as they always had. My first visitor was Josephine, apologising for the cancelled wedding rehearsal and it seemed best to leave that illusion intact.

The wedding went ahead as planned. The real Josephine, my friend Josephine Bingley, stood next to Cedric Winstanley as they made their vows at a completely undamaged altar. Not a sign of the chaos that had engulfed me the previous night.

As always I failed to catch the bouquet but that is me to a tee, the eternal bridesmaid. I don't regret stepping neatly aside for Maggie Kemple to take the honour – the look of pure joy on her face as she clutched the flowers to her bosom made me quite tearful. I regret very little in life, with the exception, perhaps, for keeping this infernal poppet. Seeing it here in my hands I wonder why I've never been able to destroy it. I suppose it was not in me back then to take a life.

You think I have already? I don't see it that way at all. What do you suppose happened out there in that churchyard? That our Miss Fenn did not simply cease to exist. Nothing of the sort. She merely … changed.

The clock ticks on, growing louder in the silence; a warning of time's passage just as I had been aware of it that night. Tick-tick, slow, pulsing, echoed by the thready pattering at the Poppet's core. Still there. Always there. I can't leave this for my successor to deal with. That would never do.

It has to end.

I throw the vile thing into the grate and watch it burn. The smell is appalling, acrid fumes of burning hair that will take days to air out of the room. The Poppet is tinder dry after all these years in the attic so the fact that it burns so rapidly is hardly a shock. The way that it burns with limbs and torso contorting, crackling, hissing, and dying as rapidly as it had risen, that is shocking. Nothing left now but a few scraps of pulsating ash draped over the coals.

Goodbye Melissa Fenn. Your spell on Earth is finally ended.

DÆMOS RETURNS
David J Howe

If there's one good thing about living in the English countryside, it's that the weather and the scenery are changeable. One moment it can be sunny and warm, and the next drizzling and cold. It's even been known to hail in the middle of summer … and don't get me started about spring and autumn which has weather that just doesn't know what season it is.

Having a bicycle is another of the best things, especially when the weather and the scenery conspire to present a blue sky, light breeze, and attractive vistas as you cycle by.

It frees the mind too; although my mind is want to dwell on things recently past. Well, you can't really blame me. It was all somewhat out of the usual.

On this particular day I had decided to cycle to Witchwood, a little hamlet some five miles from my little cottage in Devil's End. Oh I know, I know what you're thinking … those names sound a little strange … and so they are! Add to them Covenstone, Satanhall and Abbotsburn … we live in interesting times!

The wind was in my hair and my feet were merrily pumping away at the pedals. The sun was shining. It was a lovely day. I had helped one of my friends there with some herbal remedies to assist their child to get a restful sleep and was headed back to Devil's End. As I came over the brow of the Goat's Back, I saw the sun hitting the shattered remains of St Michael's church. I came to a stop right in the middle of the road and looked at the broken masonry.

As always, my mind was whisked back to the events of the previous summer. Of a May Day which should have been full of fun and laughter and children singing and dancing, but which instead had been full of omens and evil.

I remembered that evil man. The Master they called him, but I knew him as the Reverend Magister. Not very much reverend about him, I can tell you. Then there was the film crew, out at the Devil's Hump, determined to let that crazy archaeologist dig into the ground. And on Beltane! The very night that all things spiritual and dangerous are afoot.

Of course the newspapers made good copy out of what had happened next. Horner, or whatever that archaeologist was called, was killed. Frozen to death in the tunnel. People talked of seeing moving statues, and giant hoofprints appeared in the fields. It was nearly the end of times. One of the worst moments we've ever had at Devil's End, though the fight to keep back evil never ends here.

Luckily we had a great man to help us. A scientist well versed in the arts himself. Quiquaequod I called him, but he called himself the Doctor. A doctor of what I have no idea, but knowing him, probably everything! Thanks to him, the schemes of Magister were uncovered and the whole thing ended … but what an end. With the destruction of our lovely church!

It was a sacrifice which had to be made of course. Strange forces were afoot that night, and the church was the centre. I still remember running for my life as it crumbled behind us.

Magister was taken away by the army, and the Doctor and his little assistant headed back to London or wherever they had come from, leaving the villagers to do their best to come to terms with what had happened. And it wasn't easy! It was my job as usual to try and help everyone make sense of a supernatural occurrence that really had no easy explanation behind it.

As I paused on the hill, all these things went through my mind. It had been a hellish spring in more ways than one.

I sighed, shook my head to clear away the memories of the past, and pushed off on my bike again, heading down into Devil's End. At the bottom I reached the crossroads, and from there it was just a short ride to my cottage. But standing at the corner of the road as I approached was a figure.

I blinked, and the man abruptly turned and disappeared into the trees. I squinted, trying to see movement in the woods, but there was nothing. Where had he gone?

But I *knew* who it was. It was Garvin! I was sure of it!. And I had thought I would never see him again! The little weasel of a man who had allied himself to Magister and helped him with his evil summonings.

But Garvin was dead! He had been … *vanished* I suppose you'd say … by a little demonic creature summoned by Magister. And these creatures, what were they? One of the familiar church gargoyles brought to horrific life by whatever powers Magister was using. Even now the thought of them brought a shudder to my spine.

As I passed where I was sure he had been standing, I pulled my bike into the curb. I looked carefully into the thicket of trees and bushes but there was nothing to be seen.

Perhaps I had been cycling too hard and for too long, and my eyesight was going … but no. Every witch instinct was tingling. I knew what I had seen.

After a few moments I continued into the town. I was disturbed by this strange encounter and the sunshine and birdsong could not quite chase away the shadow which I felt was following me.

That night, the village was unsettled. There was something in the air that made my friends and neighbours nervous. As I headed on my daily walk, taking in all the key areas of the place, I listened to stories of ghosts and sightings.

'Is everything all right?' I asked my dear friend Ruben Greenwood as I passed his cottage. The man was standing by his gate, looking out across the green as though he had seen a ghost.

'Sure, Miss Hawthorne,' he said. 'It's just that … I thought I saw …'

Ruben fell quiet, unwilling to continue. He knew of my

powers, and he was one of the few people in the village I could turn to moments of extreme danger.

'You know, you can always tell me anything …' I said.

'One of the barmaids said the old innkeeper, Bert, had been seen pottering in the cellar of The Cloven Hoof.' Ruben continued.

Bert was another person who had disappeared on that fateful Beltane.

'Did anyone else see him?' I asked.

Ruben revealed that other people had reported seeing friends, loved ones, shadowy figures walking in the street, or half-glimpsed in reflected moonlit windows. Whenever these phantoms were seen, they vanished into the air as soon as full attention was turned to them.

I discovered that even old Mrs Grendel was seen tending to her flower garden, but everyone knew that she had passed some time ago: killed by her husband or so the gossip went.

Ruben himself had seen Squire Winstanley striding through the streets as though he still owned the place …

After that the door to my little cottage was knocked on so often that I thought the hinges would break. People called on me to report what they had seen, or what they thought they had seen. People long-dead walking the streets, coming back to life … and then disappearing again like dew on a spring morning.

I could dismiss some of the reports, but not Peter Thomson. Peter came to me late in the day to tell me of his dead wife's return. Peter was about my age by then, late forties, and as handsome a man as the village had seen.

Peter was a widower, but we were friends and saw each other socially from time to time. He and Marj had moved in just after the Beltane, when the village was getting back on its feet. They were a friendly couple but it wasn't long after that Marj became ill. She had been a sweet lady, unassuming and kind. She always had a good word for everyone. I remembered her speaking out for a group of kids who had been caught scrumping apples – and that of course brought to mind my own apple thief, Rhad and Marj was always first in line if someone needed any help. It had been a sad, dark day when she succumbed to a fever that had gripped her for several weeks. Watching her weaken and fade away had been terrible, but the doctors had been helpless, and even my potions and spells seemed to have no effect. Her death was a total mystery that was put down to natural causes. I had always wondered about it – not with any real suspicion of foul play in the material sense, but suspected some in the supernatural sense. Though I could never prove it or find anyone in the village to be suspicious of.

'I tell you it was her,' Peter insisted as we sat in my living room, steaming cups of herbal tea in our hands. 'She was standing there, large as life.'

'But it can't have been her,' I explained as gently as I could. 'Marj was taken from us, you remember that?'

'Course I do,' he said. 'Couldn't forget a thing like that now, could I? Even went up to the churchyard to check that her grave was still there.'

I nodded and smiled sympathetically, 'And was it?'

Peter nodded. 'Sure was. Undisturbed it was, and with her name written on the headstone as it always has been.'

Eventually, when Marj passed away, and the village mourned – her loss was genuinely felt by everyone. I left my suspicions at her graveside, there was no need for querying her death, it would only have led to greater pain for all. Especially for Peter.

But now she had been seen again and by her husband, I was beginning to wonder if the dead were returning in order to tell us something important..

I wondered what could possibly be happening.

'Let's walk,' I suggested, and let Peter help me up out of my chair. He got my coat, and we walked around the green. I liked Peter, liked him a lot. I'd often wondered if I should pluck up courage to talk to him more often, and now fate had handed me this chance … and me, with my line of business … I should know that when fate steps in … well … it wouldn't be right to ignore her now would it?

So Peter and I walked and we talked … and we talked … and as the afternoon drifted into evening we sat outside The Cloven Hoof and conversed some more. Peter provided the drinks – glass of beer for himself, and an elderflower cordial for me. I avoided alcohol because it dulls the senses. It's not something I've ever enjoyed … at least not since Victor … and I wasn't going to make such a stupid mistake again.

And so we spent the evening drinking and chatting … and there was some laughter there as well, despite the stories which were circulating, and at the end of the day, Peter saw me back to my door.

He said goodnight and I watched him turn and walk back down my path. I smiled. Perhaps life was about to get better. It had been such fun talking to him.

Peter and I saw a lot of each other over the next few days. He would come calling with more stories of people who had been seen around the village. I would cast the runes and always see impending disaster but not how or when or why …

I was concerned of course, but Peter's company was very pleasant, and although I couldn't really *sense* any catastrophe heading our way I knew that the runes were usually correct, so I was on my guard.

But then one day, my cat, Rhad, vanished.

Now this might not seem like too big a deal, but Rhad had been my more or less constant companion, and for him to just disappear was very unusual. I know that some cats, especially toms, do roam. But not Rhad. He was never far from me. And so, I became immediately concerned when he didn't respond to my call.

I searched the village for him of course, checked all the obvious places. I even consulted the Talisman of Mercury, but to no avail. There were no clues as to where he had gone and my neighbours all reported not having seen him that day at all. Even those that he regular visited, as cats were want to do.

There was a palpable absence of feline in my cottage. I could *feel* that he was missing and it made the air feel stranger.

I was so concerned that I mentioned he was lost to Peter when he came over that evening.

'But I saw Rhad only today,' he said with surprise in his eyes. 'Up by the church.'

'Are you sure,' I asked. 'Cats can look similar to each other.'

'It was definitely your Rhad,' said Peter. 'Same tortie cat. Same knowing stare. Couldn't mistake him.'

I was suddenly gripped with an icy fear. If Rhad was still around but not staying with me, there had to be something very odd happening. And why would he be near the church? I had never known him to show much interest in the place, especially since last year.

'It's the one place I didn't think to look! We need to go and see if he's still there,' I said, making my mind up. Prevaricating was not going to help.

I stood and set down my teacup. I picked up my reticule and wards of protection from the sideboard and headed to the hallway to fetch my wrap.

'Come on then,' I said. 'I hope you're not expecting me to do this on my own!'

With a sigh, Peter joined me. He was that sort of a man. He would never leave a woman to get on with things, not if there was some help or aid he could offer.

Together we left my cottage and headed over to the small hill off the village green where the church had once stood.

As we approached the ruins, I could see the shattered remains of the gravestones poking up from the ground. The village had buried its dead here for eons, far longer than even I had been around. Some of the graves went back to the tenth century ... the place had real history. Though not all of that history was in the realms of normality.

I picked my way through some fallen masonry, noting that even after less than a year, nature was reasserting itself, and making the fallen stones a part of the scenery. Moss and lichen was growing strongly on the rocks, and grass and ivy had taken root all around them.

'Over here,' called Peter.

He was standing close to where the church had stood, and, beside him, descending into the earth was a flight of stone steps.

'Listen,' he said.

I stayed still, and then, faintly, I heard the sound of a cat yowl. I had accidentally stepped on the tail or paw of Rhad several times, and knew the sound instantly. It was Rhad. And he was in pain.

I looked at Peter. 'It sounds like him.'

Peter nodded, and started to descend the steps.

The brick dust and ancient mortar crunched under his feet as he went. I looked around. All was silent this close to the church. The locals never came this far – why should they? All they knew was that the church had been destroyed in some terrorist attack masterminded by Magister. They hadn't seen what I had seen … and I had done a good job of backing up that rumour whenever anyone expressed a suspicion that things had been otherwise.

I hefted my bag and felt the weight of my sturdy crystal ball inside. All was good. If anything came my way, then they would feel that on the back of their heads. I'd had to physically and psychically defend myself many times over the years. As I've said, Devil's End has always attracted evil and dangerous people had often found their way here.

I hurried down the steps, worried about leaving Peter to face whatever was down there alone. The gloom at the bottom seemed to engulf us as we entered the shadow of the church's basement, and I noted that it was colder too, the warmth of the day had not penetrating this far.

Peter stopped. He had reached the old door which blocked entry to the church's inner santum. But the door seemed to have borne the brunt of the explosion, and was cracked and shattered. Long splinters of wood hung from the hinges, and the door itself leaned at a drunken angle.

Peter pushed at it, and with a deafening squeal in the enclosed space, it twisted and fell to the floor with a clatter.

Peter shot a glance at me, and stepped over the broken

wood. A few feet farther on, and we stepped out into one of the church's basement rooms. This had been used as a storeroom at one point, and was lined with old wooden shelving. Much of the content was on the floor: old hymn books, papers, some cloths which might at one time have been altar cloths but which were now dusty and mouse-nibbled.

My eyes adjusted to the gloom and I looked around. There was a dim light filtering through the door behind us and I could see the disturbed dust floating in the beam.

I breathed out, suddenly realising that I had been holding my breath.

'Where now?' I asked, my voice quiet and yet loud in the space.

As if in reply, there was another cry from Rhad.

Peter moved towards the far wall, and, pulling at a rotten cloth which was hanging there, revealed a more ornate doorway. I had never seen this door before, or the steps that had brought us down into the bowels of the church.

The frame was of carved stone, and it rose in an impressive arch above us. The door itself was again wooden, and again was split down the centre, as though some great force had been applied to it. At the time I put this down to the happenings of the previous year. All sorts of destruction had occurred that day, hence why the church had never been reused: the damage was just too significant.

Peter pushed the door gently, and it reluctantly swung open, grating on lumps of stone and grit on the floor.

As the echoes died away, we looked through to see something of a temple!

Of course it was nothing of the sort, but that was the impression.

It was the cavern under the church. This had once been something of a tourist attraction. Known as the Witches Cavern, it was part-man-made and part natural, hewn from the stone beneath the church. It had housed several waxwork tableaux of witches through the centuries. All totally inaccurate of course, but the tourists seemed to like it.

Now the ceiling was mostly out of sight in the gloom, but there was a hole broken through and this allowed a shaft of light to pierce the darkness, illuminating part of an altar or a coffin. I could see other things there too. There were stones and rubbish all over the floor, which was shattered and buckled. Candle holders were strewn about, and statues were anywhere but where they should have been, all having fallen from their perches when the explosion rocked the church.

In one corner I could see the blood-red glint of an altar cloth, ruched up as though it had been casually thrown there.

Peter started to peer and poke into the corners, but there wasn't much to see there.

The cat yowled again, much closer this time, and we both stood still. After a moment Peter started to home in on the sound. It was coming from the other side of the cavern.

'Stay here,' said Peter. 'I don't want you to trip and hurt yourself on all of this chaos. I'll go and see if I can find him.' I didn't argue as Peter headed off across the centre of the space, through the shaft of light coming from above, and towards two large, buttressed pillars which held up the ceiling, and presumably the rest of the church above.

As he moved, my eyes scanned the room. The floor was littered with debris and rubbish and I was equally as worried that he may stumble and injure himself too. My eyes washed over the litter and then noticed a peculiar anomaly. The mess was everywhere. All except for one flagstone.

I narrowed my eyes. The flags on the floor were all cracked and at jaunty angles, as though something under the ground had tried to escape. All except for this one stone. It was square and clear of any debris. It also seemed to be level and undamaged.

A memory flashed into my mind, something about a stone, and what happened if you stepped on it. My world span and I suddenly felt Peter's hand on my arm, steadying me. I hadn't noticed him hurrying back across the room to meet me.

'Careful there, it's treacherous underfoot!'

I looked down and my feet were almost touching this

unmarked and level flag. The top of the stone was scored with a pattern of lines and runes, and I remembered. This was the keystone in the cavern, the one from which the unnatural power had emanated. I remembered lovely Sergeant Benton stepping on it and getting the pummelling of his life from the forces trapped within.

I frowned. How had I got here? I had been several feet away. I didn't remember crossing the floor. One more step and ...

'Will you look at that?' Peter noticing the flagstone for the first time. His observation pulled me back from my reverie and into the present immediate danger. 'It's intact.'

He crouched down and went to touch the markings, but I stayed his hand.

'No! Peter. No. It could be dangerous. I remember it from before.'

Peter frowned up at me. 'Dangerous? How could a stone be dangerous?'

At that moment, the atmosphere in the cavern changed. There was a deadening sensation in the air that muffled the sound of our presence. It was as though someone had cocooned us in cotton wool. The temperature dropped suddenly, and I saw my breath steam as I let out a gasp.

Peter stood.

Faintly at first, but then more definite, people started to become visible around us. Like droplets of milk falling into water, they coalesced from the air, until they surrounded us. They were eerily silent but for a throbbing sound, a gently pounding which accompanied the appearances, and I realised that it was the sound of my own heart beating.

Peter and I stood there, in that shattered cavern and watched as all the dead of Devil's End rose up to greet us.

Some shuffled silently out of the shadows, others stood watchful. Waiting.

I could feel the incessant pull and tug nagging at the base of my skull, as something tried to worm its way inside, trying to take control. I had felt this once before, when, in the village before the madness of Horner and the dig and what came later,

I had been buffeted by an immense wind. The gale had blown up from nowhere, and yet, despite the subliminal pulling treaty to submit, I called on the elementals to calm, and the wind died along with the evil force that had attempted to assault me.

Once all was still, I found PC Groom standing beside me, holding a large rock. I suspect he had been following an insinuated instruction to remove me from the equation before I managed to calm the winds and repel whatever power was being raised against me.

'What on earth is happening?' Peter whispered.

I listened to the steady hum of magic, and realised that something wanted me to step onto the flag. It needed my power. And it had summoned up these wraiths and spectres to act as my guard, hoping to ensure that I did as they wanted. Although I doubted that they could prevent us from leaving. Spirits rarely have any hold over the living, and it is only fear that gives them strength in the end. And, as my heart pounded faster I knew that fear might well be my undoing.

Peter gripped my hand. He was my rock. The only sure and trustworthy thing I had at that moment. His presence helped me steady my nerves. I am a powerful witch, and I know magic, but I'm also human, and I know what evil magic can do better than anyone. Only a fool would be arrogant in the face of such an entity.

Right then I understood all of the malevolence that had been in this place. There was something of it left. When the entity, devil, whatever it was that had been summoned, was despatched, it took the church with it, but it also left an essence behind. Something waiting in the single unsanctified stone in the cavern. The one place it could hide undetected.

Now it needed a channel, a means to escape. Some of its considerable power had bled out, creating phantoms and images of those it had taken, and those who were buried in the church grounds. Creating spectres out of people's memories and using them to talk, and spread news, all in the hope that someone with power would come and investigate.

And now I was there. I had the power. And I had been

chosen. You see Rhad had not gone missing by accident, but by design.

I looked around at all of the familiar faces. People I had known. Some of them I recognised from the business with Magister. There was Garvin again, his weasel-face grinning. Squire Winstanley was there too, smiling benignly at me.

Peter pulled me back to reality again.

'What's happening Olive?' he asked, looking around at all the phantoms. 'I can see all these people ... so many people ...'

I tried to think ... how could I get out of this?

I took a step away from the flagstone and towards the press of phantom flesh. Rather than parting before me like smoke, it was like pressing into a wall of soft mallow. It gave slightly, but then there was increasing resistance. The entity inside the stone was not going to merely let us walk away after all. I had seriously misjudged its control on the phantoms.

I pushed back hard. And it hurt. A sharp pain in my temple reminded me that this wasn't just a physical assault. There was a psychic element to it as well ... and if it was hurting me, then I could only think what it would do to Peter.

I stepped back, my heels almost touching the flag. Peter was beside me. The only step I could take was onto the tile ... which was exactly where they wanted me to go.

But I could not take that step. I could not be the channel which would release all of this evil back into the world, not after all the sacrifices which had been made to contain it before.

'Marj?' said Peter.

I was giddy and my head hurt with an impending migraine but Peter's voice filtered through the psychic attack and I looked up.

Peter's wife was standing on the other side of the cavern. She was faded but smiling at Peter. Unlike the rest of the throng which had this thread of milk-like substance through them, Marj was clear and unsullied by the evil which bound the rest of the room.

I threw a psychic ward out and my senses poured forward towards her. She appeared to be benign.

Peter was looking at her. His face was a picture of love and loss, of seeing again this woman whom he had loved so much. He smiled.

'It's Marj,' Peter said again, clenching my hand so tightly in his. 'It really is!'

The phantom of Peter's wife smiled at us, and then raised her own hand in an unmistakable gesture. *Come.*

Before I could say a word, Peter let go of my hand and stepped onto the flagstone. My throat was paralised with shock, but inside my head I screamed 'No!'

I couldn't have stopped him if I had been able to speak, and the strength had left my arm, even though I reached for him. In a split second he had taken the step and as his feet touched the stone, his body stiffened. The magical entity flooded gleefully out of the stone where it had been trapped, and suffused Peter's body.

But Peter was a good man, and he was not the channel that this evil had hoped for. Like Benton before him, Peter bent double as a million blows pummelled his body. The being sought to control him and to use him as a vehicle for its own devices.

Peter didn't cry out. He didn't scream.

His eyes widened with pain, but throughout his horrible ordeal he kept them fixed on Marj. She was his beacon. His light.

I threw my hands to my mouth and watched on, helpless and horrified.

Around me I could sense the phantoms shifting and moving. I stepped backwards, away from the horrific spectacle and felt their pressure subside. They were becoming less distinct by the second.

I looked across to where the image of Marj was still standing. She was gently smiling, her face full of compassion. I realised then that this had been the solution all along. That an insensate human had to create the circuit, and then the monster's power would be expelled. In the same way that high towers needed lightning rods driven into the earth to protect them against electrical damage, so this psychic enemy needed to be 'earthed' by a normal human.

There was a loud crack, and the cavern went momentarily dark. I saw from the corners of my eyes the surrounding phantoms lose substance and drift apart into milky strands which then thinned and vanished into the ether, leaving behind a swirl of brick dust and the vaguest smell of the grave.

The light returned, spearing from the gap in the ceiling and striking the flagstone on which Peter still stood.

He crumpled and fell into my arms and I lowered him to the floor. Beneath his feet, the flagstone was cracked right through, thin wisps of the milky substance still drifting from the fracture.

Peter's eyes closed, and I rested his head on my lap and stroked his forehead. It was all I could do. Water leaked from my eyes unchecked as I stroked his face. I could hear the sound of birdsong from outside, and the cavern seemed normal once more. No psychic pressure. No feeling of oppression. Just me, heart sore and broken over the unnecessary death of yet another innocent.

I looked up and saw that the figure of Marj was still standing, watching me. She smiled sadly, sensing my own grief.

As I watched, she lifted her arm from her side, and another shape misted into view beside her, holding her hand. It was Peter. He looked down at his hand in wonder. Then he looked over at me, sitting on the floor with his body cradled in my arms.

'I'm so sorry …' I said.

Peter smiled at me. He nodded, as if to say, 'All is well.'

Then finally he looked at Marj.

A smile crossed his face. The biggest, happiest smile that a man could ever have.

My eyes filled again with tears, and through the blur, I watched as the two figures faded from view, leaving me alone in the cavern.

I sat there for some time. Crying. Holding my friend.

It was all I could do.

After some time I pulled off my wrap and placing in down

like a cushion I eased Peter's head onto it.

By now my limbs were cramped and I pulled myself to feet with great difficulty. There was only one thing I could do, I had to notify the proper authorities of Peter's death, and that wasn't the local constabulary. Back at my cottage I had a phone number that I had been told to call in case of emergencies. Now was definitely such an emergency and I hurried back to my home, leaving Peter's body where it was.

A few hours later I heard a dull explosion. I hurried from my cottage and back towards the church.

Dust was flying up from a newly created crevasse, or so I thought, but when I reached the site I discovered that the stairway Peter and I had found had been destroyed, and was now covered.

I looked around for evidence of the special operations team that I knew had done this, but none could be seen. But there was a new sign now on the church.

It said. KEEP OUT. DANGER.

'Good,' I murmured. 'Hopefully now the evil below the church was finally put to rest. And if it wasn't then, the authorities had made it clear that no one should disturb this site again.

I turned my back on the church, hoping that they had at least removed Peter's body, and would give him the burial he deserved, and I saw a beige beret lying on the floor.

I smiled, nodding my head with this confirmation that all was now well. I trusted these people with my life. And they trusted me to continue to be the buffer between the portal at Devil's End, and the world. We made a good team.

HAWTHORNE BLOOD
Raven Dane

I did my best to gather some May blossom at the first light of dawn, ancient folk ways that seem so antiquated now to people wired up to this fast, brash computer age. This was always going to be a sad Beltane but I had always honoured my namesake, the sacred hawthorn tree growing in front of my cottage. A tree so beloved of the Goddess, that I do not cut the branches during the rest of the year. The tree rewarded me by leaving low hanging boughs where the pretty white, pink-tipped blossom was easy to collect. Some country people still know the hawthorn as the faerie tree, such a gnarled, thorny beauty. One that can live to a great age, and can be found growing in the wildest and harshest of places. A bit like me! Well, at least the great age and gnarled part.

I smiled at bittersweet thoughts of past May Days. The distant days of my youth, when I was so young and supple, I could climb, stretch and gather the blossom high up in the branches, doing my best to avoid the thorns. I accepted their sharp presence as a blessing, they were protective barbs for the sacred trees that safeguarded my home … the village. I remember Poppy urging caution down below the branches, the memory of her sweet voice rising up and into my heart.

The shears felt heavier than ever this year. Arthritis plagued my hands with worsening pain and growing weakness and made the tool leaden and cumbersome. Of course, I could have asked for help, there were still people in the village steeped in the old ways, knew how to help and respect an old woman, an old wise woman … a witch. But it felt an imposition this year, something I would never do. And I had my visitor.

I paused to rest briefly, so soon after gathering the blossom, this was not good. Taking a deep breath of the cool spring morning air, I watched the sun rise through a low lying mist. The atmosphere sparkled before the mist dissolved into oblivion leaving only a short lived silver rime on the grass and leaves. This was a blessed morning where nature showed off its charms and fleeting, ever changing beauty. In this uncertain world and at my great age, it was always a privilege to witness the birth of another day.

My task done, I returned to the cottage. I was so tired. A bone deep exhaustion of mind, body and soul but I had to carry on. This had to be done.

I put down the full wicker basket of May blossom on the front doorstep. Once, young girls from villages would bathe their faces on May Day in an infusion of blossom and freshly drawn spring water. I did that too, with Poppy, so long ago now. It was supposed to give us long lasting beauty! Well, there was no harm in trying. In other, happier years, more blossom would decorate the maypole in the centre of the village green. Decades ago, the village girls used to come here to collect the flowers directly from my tree because they had been blessed by the Goddess. Not anymore, but I had to have them out ready – just in case.

I looked out of the window as the morning brightened. All misty memories of the night banished. Instinctively, I grabbed my ankh necklace, a source of solace in the past. I needed it more than ever now. The toll of so many years of life was making my body ache and fail. My mind was not as sharp as it had been. The time to pass on the grimoire was growing ever nearer, yet …

I picked up my Book of Shadows, my witch's daily diary and held my pen. My thoughts were confused, conflicting. I spoke out loud.

'Should I put this incident in the diary? Or in the grimoire itself? Who now will ever read it? Some stranger, who'll dismiss my account as the ramblings of a fool? One who lived her life in the deluded belief she was a witch. Yet, if the goddess shows mercy and there is one to follow me, then my heir must know. Must understand!'

I looked back out of window to see the village green and the hawthorn blossoms that surround it in full bloom, all bathed in warm morning sunshine and graced with a cloudless azure sky. Any other time this would have been a memorable May Day. Unlike this one that has brought such sadness and horror.

'My time as the protector of Devil's End is almost over.'

Nothing has made that more certain than what I had faced that fateful morning. That I needed help proved to be my weakness, my vulnerability. I had hated dragging my dear old friend, Ruben Greenwood, into the unfolding nightmare, but what else could I do?

Ruben is even older than me, bless him. He looks after the protective circle of hawthorn, rowan and yew hedge and the many magnificent oak trees that surround the village. A hard job now, so many newcomers are settling into the village and many want to cut it down 'to improve the view'! If only they knew what would come into sight should they succeed in breaking the outer circle!

Ruben's family were of very old village stock, from the very first, still pagan, Anglo Saxons to settle here and build the village. His bloodline, like mine, is even older than that. The early Saxon settlers interbred with the indigenous British folk. An ancient people who also knew of the danger from the portal, and its evil. They did all they could to keep it closed. How can we old fools ever explain this to the modern generation? But how can we stop doing all we can to prevent it? Duty and destiny bind us.

An unwelcome memory interrupted my discourse, a vision of the infamous Devil's Hump and I let out a deep, heartfelt sigh of distress and sorrow. The site of that arrogant fool of an archaeologist, Professor Gilbert Horner and his ill-fated excavation. He thought he had discovered the barrow tomb of a Bronze Age warrior chieftain from 800BC. An understandable assumption, I suppose, but so very wrong. We villagers did not know what it contained but it were certain it was not an ancient burial. He would not be told and like even the Doctor, dismissed our fears as idiotic local superstition. I did all I could to warn them, Horner's team, the BBC broadcasters covering the excavation, the Doctor and his companions to no avail. I was just a dotty, foolish woman to them, an object of pity and scorn.

In fact, the barrow contained the Dæmon Azal and his spacecraft. When it was opened, poor Professor Horner was instantly frozen to death. He did not deserve that horrible fate, none of the victims of evil released by the portal ever did. But I digress. My mind is more inclined to wander now.

As I have said, I needed an heir to my legacy, and hope had come but a few days earlier when there was a light tap on my front door.

I wasn't expecting anyone and so I looked through the front window, and saw a young woman standing at the door. She had dark hair and from what I could make out of her pale features, she was young and beautiful, maybe eighteen or nineteen? I often had tear-streaked girls looking for urgent readings after their boyfriends had left them, so this was not that unusual.

I opened the door and the girl greeted me with a warm, confident smile lit by a pair of startling green eyes. I had a flare of recognition. The girl reminded me of Poppy. Could it be that these were Hawthorne eyes?

I stepped back from the door and waved my hand, making it obvious that she was being invited inside.

My heart pounded. Had the time come? Could this young woman be the answer to my prayers? Was she, as every instinct in my body screamed, a Hawthorne I could pass my legacy onto?

She shook my hand and a shiver of recognition touched my soul. I hesitated, puzzled. There was more to her than her outward appearance. Did she really have the blood of the Old

Ones mixed in her veins? That was never certain to be a good thing. But there was definitely Hawthorne blood in there too. I was too excited to care about anything else.

'Please sit,' I said, my thoughts tumbled in an unruly mess, not knowing what to say first I sank down in to my chair opposite her.

The girl smiled and put me at ease.

'Let me make us both a cup of tea, and then we can talk,' she said.

Over tea and biscuits, I learned the girl's name.

'I'm Bryony,' she said.

She was the daughter of a deceased, very distant cousin.

'For a long time, I didn't know who I was,' Bryony explained. 'From the day I was born I was passed from foster home to foster home. As soon as I turned 18, I was able to know the truth.'

Now that she was of age to find her own path in life, Bryony had learnt who her parents were. Up until then the poor girl had no permanent home or real family to call her own.

'You were never adopted?' I asked.

'No,' she said and this gave me a small sliver of concern. I was surprise because I thought that in this country there was no shortage of loving adoptive homes for healthy little babies.

I was curious, but I decided there was plenty of time to find out more.

'What brings you here?' I asked her. I dare not assume what my heart already knew.

'I was drawn to Devil's End by many nights of powerful visions.'

I waited for her to continue but I knew she had been brought to me by a sense of overwhelming need and destiny.

I was overcome with joy because I had already convinced myself she was the one. Bryony was the heir who would look after the villagers and keep watch over Devil's End.

My conviction wasn't based on hope alone. While Bryony was busy washing up the teacups in my kitchen, I unlocked the cabinet and saw the glow of the grimoire as it recognised the presence of another Hawthorne, It had reached out to her as it had once reached out to me. I was overjoyed. Someone else would be able to guard against the dark forces that tried to breach the portal at Devil's End and I could finally have the peace I now craved.

I held my excitement in check. There was no need to rush, to frighten the poor girl away. I had to know the secrets of her heart before I could decide whether she had the strength and resolve to carry on the often arduous and always dangerous family duty.

Instead we sat, at ease with each other's company, and Bryony told me more about her young life. It had not been a happy childhood and so my sympathy for her grew.

Later that morning, we took a stroll around the village. Beltane was soon, the joyous feast of May Day was almost upon us. A group of lads were tidying the village green, one whistled as he noticed my beautiful young companion. She did not get angry with this but laughed and waved back in their direction. I took it as youthful confidence.

I should have seen it as a warning. But instead I welcomed her to the village, and to my home, with open arms.

That night, Bryony insisted on going to The Cloven Hoof alone. On our walk, she had learned that rehearsals had begun for the celebrations that night, and the village pub would be full of young people, dancers, singers and musicians. Far more entertaining than a night listening to the wittering of an old woman and I had no power over her; she was a young adult and still a stranger to me. It was some comfort that I knew every one of the local men. Some I had even helped deliver into the world. I had mixed up enough lotions and potions to sort out their scrapes and sniffles, illnesses and gave advice with family problems. I trusted them. Bryony would be safe.

'Did you have a good time, my dear?' I asked as she entered the parlour.

To her surprise, I was still awake when she returned at

midnight, her green eyes glowing, and an unsettling smile of triumph on her face that gave me a shiver of unease. No doubt she had expected this old woman to be long taken to her bed. I was sitting in my favourite, comfy old armchair, battered and saggy like me! I was writing in my diary, my witch's Book of Shadows, always a private notebook. I closed and locked it with a curious premonition to be wary. What had changed over so few hours? Most certainly, that wild, knowing expression as she walked through the door gave me tremendous pause. She had none of the innocence of our first encounter. Earlier that day, her perfume had been light, a fragrant memory of wild roses. Now something about her persona was feral and earthy and not in a good way. There was a scent closer to decay and corruption than to fertile earth, a cradle for life.

The changes in her from that night confirmed my suspicions: there was no doubt in my mind that Bryony was not totally human, that she indeed came from the Old Ones, but what nature of Earth Elemental was in her ancestry? What did she want from me?

The next morning, I got up early, leaving Bryony to sleep. I had a posset of dried herbs to give to an elderly visitor. It would be used as a tea that would ease her rheumatism. The poor lady was in such pain and modern medicine was not helping. And, no matter what was happening in my own life, I had a duty to help anyone in need.

I did not have to venture far before realising there was serious trouble in the village. I could sense the fear and distress before speaking to anyone. I found dear old Ruben Greenwood standing in a huddle of village men, none newcomers. Their faces were ashen, their manner subdued, all had removed any flat caps and stood heads bowed.

'It's not good news, Miss Hawthorne,' Ruben mumbled, 'we've lost one of our young uns.'

'What's happened? I asked.

'Robbie Merrow has gone missing!'

Robbie had not returned from the pub the night before. I knew that he was a good lad, with an ailing mother to care for.

His disappearance was so unlike him, we all sensed something bad had happened.

I joined the search party for as long as my aching joints would allow. It was as if the boy had left the village without a word, yet his other clothes and possessions still remained, including his pride and joy, a treasured classic MGB roadster sports car. If he had left the village it would have been behind the wheel of that gleaming, red beauty.

On returning to my cottage, Bryony had made herself toast and coffee. She showed no sign of being aware of my fatigue and anxiety. Nor did she even so much as offer me a cup of tea. She had settled into my home too easily, a fact that I noticed but took as a behaviour wrought from her unsettled upbringing.

I sat down and asked if she remembered seeing the missing boy at the pub.

Bryony shrugged with cold indifference. 'All those yokel men look the same to me. A bunch of lumpen, red-faced turnips. Why should I remember any of them?'

Such rudeness and distain. Was there any point in mentioning to her that young Robbie had won a place at Oxford University? That he was thought by many to be the best looking young man in the village and considered quite a catch?

As she tore into her toast, ripping through the thick bread and strawberry jam, the image of sharp teeth rending flesh came into my mind. An image which troubled me deeply. What a strange thing to think about in the presence of a pretty young woman? A Hawthorne woman at that. Yet I found myself wanting to be away from her, from her strong personality and persistent questioning. It was as if she knew my time on this earthly plane was growing short, that I yearned for a successor to protect the village and the world beyond. There was something disquieting about her eagerness to know more about me. Yet she was far more interested in my witchy trappings than my personal history.

My mind was also too full of worry about poor Robbie and his distraught mother. In earlier times, I would have remained helping with the search but I was too old, too weak. I knew in bad times, the villagers always pulled together, Mrs Merrow would not want for supportive company. Instead I remained in my home as Bryony spent the day asking more and more detailed questions about my life. She was curious about my treasures … My crystal ball, my bottles of herbs, and the talismans against evil above the doors and windows.

'The talismans are for protection,' I paused my narration and glanced up to the silver pentacle above the nearest window, one of many defensive talismans against evil, as if reassuring myself it was still in place. Such a shame so many modern people do not understand what it means, confusing a blessed, protective symbol of good with devil worship and other nonsense. At the time I thought what harm was there in telling her some of the ways of a wise woman? She could pick it all up in any New Age book of modern witchcraft. At least my lore was genuine. Much out there was created by cynical types jumping on the popular bandwagon of spiritual growth in order to make money. Such is life these days. But as the next day wore on, her manner became more strident, more demanding, wanting deeper, more powerful knowledge.

This impatient talk, or interrogation, wearied me and pleading my great age, I hid in my bedroom.

By some deep instinct I knew what was coming next, Bryony would want the grimoire. Despite my longing for her to be the Hawthorne heir some small voice of reason held me back and I had locked the cabinet and hidden the key when she was out of the room. Thankfully there were many interruptions to that awful day. People came to my door, asking me if there was any news of poor Robbie. Some of his friends, all young village girls, asked for my help locating him with my scrying mirror. I remember some relief amid this dreadful situation, something useful at last that I could do to help with the search.

So of course I agreed and promised Robbie's friends I would let them know if I found anything to help.

Once they left, Bryony watched fascinated while I prepared to meditate and gaze into the pure crystal surface. But before my mind was clear enough to look, the mirror was snatched from my hand by some invisible force and smashed to the floor. The frame was buckled and the glass shattered into a myriad of tiny, sharp shards, all of its magic lost forever. Bryony appeared as shocked as I was. Her tears flowed as freely as mine. Her concern seemed so genuine that I felt a twinge of guilt and I began to doubt my own misgivings.

That night Bryony went to bed early and I left the cottage to seek out Ruben Greenwood who like so many other villagers had gathered at The Cloven Hoof.

I entered the pub, looking around at the villagers there. The atmosphere within was subdued and solemn. Few spoke above a hushed murmur and no fire had been lit in the pub's wide inglenook. That night it was a place of gathering, not relaxation and companionship. I pitied any newcomer or visitor being jolly and noisy in there tonight. Living in the shadow of the portal, gave the old local families little tolerance of levity in troubled times.

I found Reben in his favourite seat close to the unlit fire. He did not seem surprised to see me and rose to greet me, his face sober like the other villagers.

Taking Ruben outside, well out of earshot of the others, I told him my fears and feelings. It was such a comfort to discuss such matters with a person who would believe without question, so unlike the Doctor and the team of archaeologists when the village was under the thrall of Azal. Ruben had also lived through those dark days and was a trusted ally.

'A bad business,' he muttered, knowing I would agree. This was not a time for idle speculation or optimism … not in Devil's End. We were survivors, Ruben and I, witnesses to other grim times. 'Do you know what got that poor lad?

I shook my head. Suspicions ran amok through my mind, but they were groundless, as tenuous as dreams and idle thoughts. We needed something more to go on, even if it was most likely to be poor Robbie's body.

I returned to my cottage, to find to my relief Bryony was as good as her word and had indeed gone to bed. From the doorway, I watched her sleep, a deep slumber that looked so peaceful, so innocent. Again, I chided myself for my suspicions. If only that scrying mirror had not broken, I could have discovered the truth about Robbie Merrow and put everyone's mind at rest.

Not everything mysterious that happened in Devil's End had a grim reason behind it. Most of the time, life went on just like in any rural community. I found myself desperately rationalising the situation, as if this was just an ordinary village like the neighbouring ones. Quiet havens of rural serenity like Bounders Green and The Lees, but for every ordinary place there was also a Satanhall or a Witchwood – names which suggested at their origins as locations of darker intent. It was just as likely the lad had got bored with village life or worn out by the responsibility of caring for his ailing mother had disappeared for a while. If I had been younger, more active, I might have known, offered him respite care, given advice.

Returning to my bed, I did my best to sleep but it was fitful, the dreams lurid and frightening. I must have cried out in the throes of a nightmare because I discovered Bryony standing over me. I gave a little cry of alarm, a sign of weakness that filled me with self-loathing. She must not know of my suspicions.

'Poor love, you are having a dreadful night,' she soothed, her voice soft and sweet, nearly innocent but for a glint of coldness in her beautiful Hawthorne eyes. 'Let me make you a hot chocolate or a soothing tisane.'

I struggled to rise, old age is such a mixed blessing, the gift of wisdom and the curse of painful, weakening joints and fatigue. I sensed none of that wisdom now, I was nothing but a confused, fearful old woman.

'So kind of you, my child,' I muttered and managed what I hoped was a genuine-looking warm smile of gratitude. 'It was just a silly dream. I must have had one piece too many at supper of that delicious ripe Stilton cheese that Mrs Ryefield gave me last week. When you are as old as I am, little pleasures are there to be savoured but best not overindulged in.'

'A gentle fruit tea then,' Bryony said with an unmistakable

satisfied tone. 'Hot chocolate will be far too rich and we don't want you having more nightmares.'

As she left to head for the kitchen, I shuddered, my already thin, old blood now watered by the ice of growing fear. What could this young woman know of nightmares? Of a lifetime living with them hidden into the very fabric of Devil's End, of the portal to evil that constantly sought a breach to emerge into our world. The portal was also a magnet to the malign forces that were already at loose. One of those forces could be here, now, sheltered beneath my roof. I had to know the truth but what to do with such knowledge was beyond me now. My head sank back into my pillows, my hand grasped around the silver ankh around my neck, '*Isis, Danu, Gaia, our dear Mother, protect me.*'

It did not take Bryony long to prepare and bring me a mug of steaming tea, my own blend of chamomile, valerian, linden and honey. An aroma I had known since a child, one so familiar I instantly recognised something extra added to the mixture. One I most certainly did not use, or even stock. She had added some distilled essence of thorn apple. A highly toxic plant that would induce an extreme thirst to ensure I finished all the tea. A wicked thing to do. I could not drink this. It would send me into a deep, coma like sleep, one that I may never awaken from. Any last, desperate, lingering thoughts that Bryony was nothing more than a sweet young woman, my family, the long hoped for heir to my Hawthorne legacy, were dashed. Something dwelled within her that was as evil as anything that had ever spewed from the portal. A determined, cunning one too. She pushed the mug into my hands, then sat on a nearby chair, waiting for me to drink it.

'Bless you, Bryony. That is so kind and well done for choosing the best blend for a peaceful night's rest. I will wait until it has cooled down before enjoying it.'

I placed the steaming brew on my bedside table. Next to my silver framed photograph of Poppy. *Wherever you are, my angel, I need you now.*

'There is no call for you to lose any sleep, my child. Off to bed with you and thank you again.'

'Not until I see you drink up all your tea, I want to make sure you have a restful night and no more bad dreams.

My nightmare sat before me, in the form of a lovely young woman. Long dark hair swept back in a neat ponytail, the very picture of demure modesty. She needed no make up to highlight her pale, perfect skin, the beauty of her gilt-flecked eyes. Had I ever thought those eyes radiated gentleness, warmth? They were as cold as that of a snake or shark. This was a game to her, a predator toying with its victim. I knew that if I made too much fuss about not drinking it, she would become suspicious that I knew her intentions. If I drank it, I would be doomed. This was a time for some intervention, from the spirits of earth, air and water that I had communicated with since a child. Only they were capricious entities from their own dimension, their own time scale. Their aid could never be relied on, but still I prayed from the depth of my soul for help.

Downstairs, I heard the familiar creak of an old wooden door opening: the heavy, iron-bound one to my small cellar, where I stored my dried herbs, roots, autumn's apples in barrels ready to eat, gifts of wine. I feigned alarm but there was no mistaking the glance of annoyance on Bryony's face as her plan to drug me was interrupted.

'I am sure it is nothing,' I said. 'Just next door's fat, old tom cat doing his late night rounds of neighbouring cottages on the scrounge for food. Ginger George is quite the character.'

Nonsense of course, the solid oak door was far too heavy for any moggy to open. I doubted even a tiger could open it. Bryony stood up. Whatever it was, she was not afraid. Why would she be? She really was not all human and our unknown visitor downstairs had every reason to be afraid of her. Muttering reassurances in a voice tight with frustration, she went down to investigate. I did not have much time, but enough to tip all the mixture out of my bedroom window, whispering an apology to the holly bush beneath. I heard her searching downstairs, uttering foul, unlady-like oaths and by the time she returned, I had already lain back into my pillows, eyelids leaden as I feigned being overwhelmed by sleep.

'This old house is full of mystery, Bryony,' I murmured, my words slurring. 'Not all my visitors can be seen but always mean no harm.'

I saw through my half closed eyes that she had picked up the mug, inspecting it.

'Utterly delicious, my dear,' I continued, 'but perhaps a tad less honey next time?'

She smiled, kissed my forehead and left me in peace, content her plan had succeeded.

What had opened the cellar door? I would never know, but I am certain one of my ethereal friends had indeed come to my aid. I waited for what seemed to be an eternity in bed, not daring to make a move. I could hear Bryony moving about downstairs but I suspected she was waiting to make sure I was asleep before attempting anything surreptitious. I was right to be cautious, after a while longer, I heard her return up the stairs and enter my bedroom. I was able to feign a good show of being in a deep sleep, complete with realistic snoring. She seemed satisfied with this and went away. Again I waited before putting on my softest wool slippers. The creaking wooden floorboards in my cottage had served well over the centuries but were not conducive to sneaking about. I paused halfway down the stairs. I had a good view of my living room and plenty of light from the still glowing hearth. Bryony had been searching for the hidden cabinet key, leaving a mess of open drawers and pushed aside books. I could feel her mood as a wave of anger and frustration that filled the room, as tangible as a sharp, cold wind. Glad of my crocheted shawl, I continued to watch her antics.

Swearing the coarsest oaths I'd ever heard to come from a young woman, she clawed at the cabinet with her long, red-painted fingernails. Unnaturally strong, like talons, they shredded the ornate, painted wood. I winced at the destruction. That had been a wedding gift to my great, great grandmother from her handsome Romani husband. I had always cherished it, a gift made from love and the fulfilled promise of their long, happy marriage. Still unable to prise open the door, Bryony stormed down to the cellar to find something stronger. I was so tempted to rush down and lock her in but common sense kicked in. I would never get down the stairs and across the room in time, unlike in my agile youth, and what would I do once she was locked in? A ridiculous notion but one that showed how fearful I was of this young woman.

Bryony came back up into the room, wielding a crowbar. This could open the antique cabinet and I steeled myself to fight her if she tried to leave with the precious grimoire. A conflict that would not end well for me, but the Hawthorne legacy had to be protected. With a few, strong attempts, the cabinet door yielded to her efforts and the grimoire was within her grasp.

At first it glowed, as it had when Bryony had first arrived, the light that had given me so much forlorn hope. She reached down to remove the tome from its place of shattered safety but leapt back with a blood curdling, inhuman shriek. In agony as if burned by fire or acid, she gazed in fury at her hand, glowing with an ethereal white light, one that I knew would not harm the rightful keeper of the grimoire. For the first time in many, long centuries, the book had to protect itself from a Hawthorne heir. Cursing again, she did her best to minimise the damage caused by her clumsy, frantic search … just in case. She had expected I would succumb to her poison. The village would mourn the loss of its wise woman, but no doubt accept it to be a natural passing from extreme old age. Bryony would gain the cottage and contents but not the grimoire. It would never allow her to possess it. That at least gave me some satisfaction. I sneaked back upstairs and pretended to be asleep again … what a surprise I would give the fiend sheltering under my roof in the morning.

If Bryony was shocked at seeing me already awake and enjoying breakfast the next morning, she hid it well. I continued the charade.

'Thank goodness, you missed the excitement last night, my child,' I said, pouring her a cup of tea. 'While we were sound asleep, safe in our beds, we had an unwelcome visitor. Some silly young man no doubt, ransacking the living room to pocket valuables.'

She looked suitable shocked.

'How dreadful! Did they get away with much?'

I laughed. That morning I could win an Oscar for my acting skills.

'There is no price anyone could put on my things. Useless, eccentric knick knacks and trinkets of no value to a desperate thief with an expensive habit to fund. But a precious legacy to a Hawthorne witch, items gathered over millennia from the dawn times of humans dwelling on these islands.'

This seemed to satisfy Bryony and we settled down to the pretence of a normal breakfast and made small talk about burglars and ideas for getting better security. I could sense the disappointment over my survival seeping from her dark soul. The danger from my young blood relative was far from over.

The next few days passed without incident, it was so difficult for me. My ancient nerves had never been so stretched, living with this murderous creature and keeping up the pretence that all was well. Suspicious at first, Bryony seemed to relax after her failed attempt at stealing the grimoire. I had no doubt she would try again. The power and knowledge it contained was too great for her to walk away, that she had Hawthorne blood gave her a powerful claim.

As we met over breakfast on the fourth day since the incident, I could see changes in her. Her face looked pinched, pallid. Knowing her fondness for red meat, I had rustled up a cooked breakfast of toast, beef sausages and bacon, hoping to quell any hunger building up within her hybrid body. She devoured it like a starving animal but the meal did nothing to satisfy what inner urge was troubling her. This was bad, very bad. Bryony was a predator. Something … someone would die to serve her urgent needs.

'I am going out,' she announced, a petulant edge to her voice as if daring me to challenge her.

I smiled, another Oscar winning performance.

'Well, of course, my dear. Why would a young girl like you

want to be cooped up with a boring old biddy! You must be bored stiff with all my folk tales and herbal recipes by now. It is a lovely day, a nice walk around Devil's End will do you good, put some colour back into your cheeks.'

A risky ploy but I gambled she needed the cover of darkness to do her brand of evil, I needed time to research exactly what she was, to find a way of defeating her. I waited until she had left the cottage and watched in which direction she had headed. Good. The opposite direction to Ruben's nearby cottage on the green. Bringing the grimoire with me, I headed for my good friend's home. I hated dragging him into this nightmare but he was my most trusted ally and one who would accept whatever I told him as the truth without question.

Hours passed, as I studied the grimoire and Ruben surfed the internet, if that is the right word. I have never used a computer and I was impressed by the old man's proficiency in this wonder of modern life. At the end of our studies, we had come to a frustrating brick wall. With no physical evidence of young Robbie Merrow's fate, we had nothing to work on. What Bryony was or what she harboured within was still a mystery.

'She looks hungry, that at least I do know.'

Ruben glanced up at me from his computer, his normally jovial face, wrinkled like a sun-ripened apple had paled.

'Then we do not have any time left. We must act tonight.'

I returned home, a chill in my bones that had nothing to do with the weather. Bryony had not returned and a foolish, optimistic thought invaded my mind. That she had left my home for good, her plan to take the grimoire thwarted. A cowardly thought though. If she had departed from Devil's End, she would destroy other lives elsewhere. It was my duty to stop her … whatever the cost to me. Courage was hard to gather, I had never felt so vulnerable, so feeble in body, so low in spirit. Had I found a true heir of Hawthorne blood, these drawbacks would have been as nothing. If my time had come, I could accept it; move on to the Summerlands with a fulfilled and happy soul.

I was so deep in my doom-laden thoughts, I did not hear

Bryony return. I had sat by my hearth, a small apple wood fire lit despite the afternoon sun streaming into my living room, adding an extra brightness to the pentacle and crystals hanging in the window. As the sunbeams sent rainbows from the crystals dancing around the room, Bryony stepped back into the shadows, as if avoiding the enchanted light. At first she looked as I had first seen her, a lovely girl on the brink of blossoming into full womanhood. Briefly, her face changed, unable to keep up the pretence. Still beautiful, her features had hardened, her eyes gleamed with an inner cold light, waves of need, of hunger radiated from her being. And then as quickly as she lost it, she recovered her composure.

'You were right, that walk did me a world of good. And I was wrong about the locals, not all of them are turnip-headed yokels. Some are quite fit!'

I managed a smile though my heart was racing with dread and foreboding. Had she found her next victim? From her gloating smile and brazen attitude to the village men, I suspected she had. There was no turning back now, for good or ill, Ruben and I had to act that night.

Bryony and I spent the day in further study of folk lore and medicine, the distraction of me departing centuries of wisdom to her at least keeping me calm. Dwelling on what was to come would weaken the resolve of the bravest young warrior, something I was most definitely not. We finished and had an early supper then I heard Bryony's bedroom door slam shut, no doubt resting before going out later, dressed to kill – literally. Though the days were lengthening, there was not much time left until dusk. I waited as long as I dared, my heart racing with anxiety, before slipping out of the back door and picking my way through the cottage garden where all my precious herbs and flowers watched as silent witnesses to this old woman's folly. The last adventure of the White Witch of Devil's End.

When I tapped on his cottage door, Ruben answered straight away, already dressed for the cold night in a wool duffel coat and tartan scarf, the inevitable flat tweed hat crammed tight on his head. It was hard not to laugh at the sight of us two frail pensioners out on a mission to defeat evil. He picked up a sack holding tools he thought might be useful, I had brought a bag of magical items with the grimoire and we stepped out into the night aware that this could be our last.

Like a pair of silly old ne'er do wells, we hid in the hedgerow, feeling like the most unlikely and oldest spies in the world. Again, something we'd laugh about if it wasn't for our worrying suspicions. The night was clear and cold for so near May Day, the stars looked harsh, as bright and sharp as my broken mirror shards. We did our best to hide our breath by wrapping scarfs over our mouths, the tell-tale vapour of dragon's breath as I called it, would betray our presence. That dawning awareness of Bryony's feral, predatory true nature made me realise she would be alert, on the look-out for would be dangers. She survived and thrived on her illusion, that she was nothing more than a lovely young woman. A desirable one.

With the homely, warm gleam from the cottages and pub surrounding the village green the only illumination to help our ageing eyesight, we watched for any sign of her. With sinking hearts, we realised our vigil was not in vain. Before long, Bryony emerged from my cottage and headed straight across the green towards the home of John Linden, another of the village's men – this one supposedly happily married. Even in the dim light I could see she had changed her clothes from the demure ones she wore around me to something very different. A simple red dress that was alluring, revealing and enhanced her perfect, slender figure.

My suspicions were being confirmed but still I was unsure of her exact nature. Brazen in her confidence, she waited on the green for her next victim to appear. We followed behind, feeling far less foolish and a great deal more fearful. The night wind was in our favour, keeping our scent and the sound of our footfall to a minimum.

The door opened after half an hour and a laughing Bryony walked arm in arm with John Linden towards an area of woodland outside the village. My throat tightened with apprehension, like Merrow, this man though older, was very handsome, full of virile, healthy life. Had her prey been female, my lack of certainty would have continued. We followed as closely as possible without being seen. She carried on, laughing and flirting with Linden as they neared a new plantation of trees, none native, none with protective properties. Grown rapidly for felling, Bryony had chosen her killing ground with care and knowledge. I wanted to shout out a warning to Linden but his glazed stare confirmed my fears, that he was spellbound, mesmerised by Bryony to obey her without question. He had become her helpless victim from the moment she had desired him.

We could do nothing at this point, no rushing in to save him. Such rash behaviour would endanger us all. We needed time to prepare, to stack the odds in our favour.

Bryony paused in a clearing, her illusion of youthful beauty glowing in the rising moonlight. She raised her arms to embrace her eager suitor. Her strange feral scent came to me on a breeze, tainted with a sulphurous reek. His reason returning and alarmed by the change in her, John Linden tried to back away, but Bryony was strong and determined. I knew she would force him to kiss her. Then she would drain his life force into herself, killing him as assuredly as she had killed poor Robbie Merrow.

My suspicions were now confirmed: she was a succubus. A remorseless female demon that preyed on men for their life energy. Yet she was part human too, of Hawthorne blood. The only heir I had. I hesitated. Perhaps the demon inside could be suppressed, controlled? I was that desperate to still believe that Bryony was the one.

Then reason, in the form of Ruben Greenwood, broke through.

'She's killing him!' he yelled.

There was no choice. I had to prevent her doing more harm. I stepped into the clearing and shouted for her to stop. The surprise was enough to make her release her grip. Linden took advantage of it and stumbled away, running back towards the village. My heart surged with relief, restoring my courage.

Her voice had changed, now a low, rasping snarl, 'Stupid

old witch,' she said. 'What are you going to do? Wave a willow wand at me? Your time has passed, Olive. One way or another, the grimoire is mine.

All pretence of being a young woman had gone. She was a glaring, spitting she-devil. Her skin had become hard scales with a gleaming, poisonous green sheen. Her fiery eyes flared with cruelty and her teeth were now curving needles, dripping with a glowing green ichor. Her carefully manicured nails became long, raking, toxin-tipped talons. A hellish creature spawned to kill to satisfy its hunger and craving to cause pain and despair. I had to hold her attention while Ruben spread a circle of entrapment around us, a ring of ashes blended from protective woods, holy waters and sacred oils.

'Bryony, I beseech you. Let go of this evil and become the Hawthorne woman you were born to be. One the grimoire will accept.'

The creature laughed, a sound so cruel and mocking that it cut deep into my heart

'What, become a weak human? A pathetic, putrid failure like you? You could not even produce an heir of your own! Of course not, what man would want anything to do with an ugly, dried up bitch like you? You are barren, pointless and unwanted, Olive, a worn out, useless husk.'

She laughed again. 'The feeble old ways are over. The next keeper of the grimoire will be powerful, unstoppable!'

'How, Bryony? How exactly is that going to happen?'

I continued, desperate to taunt her into focusing on me. 'I saw you that night. The one when you tried to kill me with thorn apple tea. Don't you think an experienced old witch would not recognise the reek of poison? I saw you break open the gypsy cabinet and try to steal the grimoire.'

My manner changed to a mocking tone. Anger focused her attention on me better than anything else.

'That went so well for you, didn't it, you stupid girl. I saw how the grimoire rejected you, a light that should have been the gentle caress of warmth and love from all of our forebears became sheer, burning agony. Revealing your inner demon to me. The grimoire will never be yours. What are you, Bryony, if you do not embrace your humanity? Nothing but a loathsome parasite, a leech that can only survive on that of others.'

The succubus's contempt grew, she was ready to spring forward, rend me to pieces with her fangs and talons.

'The stench of death hangs around you like a shroud, Olive,' she said. 'You are nothing but crippled old bones and decaying flesh.'

That was true, her words weakened by resolve just as she planned. I felt so frail, legs unable to hold me up. She would not drain my life force, what little there was left of it. Bryony's prey was always male, full of energy but she could still rend my frail body to shreds. I still had the grimoire under my arm and a curious warmth built up from it and radiated into my body. I no longer felt alone, spirit presences surrounded me, full of love. My eyes filled with tears of joy. This was the Hawthorne legacy, the true blood line that could only ever be a force for good. With my family's help, I was strong again, standing tall and defiant in the face of this usurping enemy.

'You are nothing, Bryony. No more than an empty vessel fuelled by a need you can never fulfil. I am sorry for you. The grimoire and the Hawthorne legacy can never be yours.'

I heard a wavering whisper of relief from the darkness. 'It's done, Miss Hawthorne.'

'Thank you, Ruben.' I answered as I summoned every last ounce of strength and resolve.

From within the ash circle, I began a spell of banishment, easily finding the speed to avoid her furious lunge, but not quick enough to miss her hot breath and talons raking my shawl. That was too close! Even with my spirit help, I knew the next attack could be fatal. I stepped back outside the ring of ash, gambling it would hold her. It did.

What was once Bryony tried to follow me but was pushed back as if struck by an invisible hand. The book! That same white, comforting light was now a weapon, streaming from the grimoire and holding her back. She landed, crouching in the centre of the ring, feral and deadly. She cursed and spat but could not harm us … for now. But I knew it would not take much to disrupt our fragile ash barrier. A rain shower, a gust of wind. Was the light from the book enough? I could not risk it; I had to banish her before she could escape.

As my incantations grew louder, I had to shut my mind to the succubus. Once again, she dragged up all of my frailties, mistakes and failures, threw them in my face as weapons. Her cruel words pierced my soul. Questioning everything that gave me strength as a witch. She was using truth against me, and in that truth was power. She was right, I was a failure, I had let down my forebears, had not prevented evil from threatening the world, had not provided a female heir.

I concentrated all my energy and that of my spirit helpers into one ball of positive energy and launched it at her human heart, taking no satisfaction as she crumpled onto the ground.

A thick spiral of reeking yellow vapour rose from her body, rushed around the inner circle with an ear splitting shriek before disappearing into the ground. All that was left was a pile of charred human bones and burnt scraps of Bryony's clothing. A heart-breaking end to a young life had it not been for the great harm she had done and would continue to do to other innocent lives.

Ruben and I buried the remains as deep as we could within the protective circle. A hideous task but we had no choice. Yet again I can recall the sound of the spade cutting into the earth, the carnal reek of what was once Bryony. Poor Robbie was buried somewhere in this plantation, the killing ground of the succubus. I would have to leave it to Ruben and the other village men to find his body and inter him in hallowed ground.

I returned to the wood at dawn on the Eve of Beltane to make the banishment permanent. For now the men of Devil's End were safe.

Back inside the safety of my cottage I looked up at the window and saw the village green, forlorn in its emptiness. Not a soul on the lush, green sward. Even the birds had deserted it.

Of course, the villagers were too distressed to raise the May Pole. People were not ready for the joyous festival of Beltane.

Not this year. Not with Robbie Merrow's funeral to attend. They'd found what was left of him. Exposure they said to the police and coroner.

The folk of Devil's End know death too well. They know when it is unnatural. They want to consecrate his soul as soon as they can and wisely so. The spiritual contamination by a succubus can carry on, even after the death of her victims.

My folly is such a heavy burden. I'm such a stupid old woman! I was so eager to accept Bryony as my heir. So desperate, I did not notice that the grimoire did not glow warm with welcome of her arrival. It had shone cold in warning. Maybe if I had not been so concerned with my own need, that poor boy would still be alive and we would fill the village green to celebrate the May Day. But no. Today, they will stay away. Today, they will keep the company of grief and bury him.

The legacy of Hawthorne blood is a bitter one. Without generations of vigilance, this sad scene would be commonplace, not just in Devil's End but all over this land.

I have to stay strong, focused for as long as possible. For when I am gone, will anyone be here to carry on? All these sacrifices. My tales are done. And I am tired.

EPILOGUE
Sam Stone

On the morning following my biggest disappointment, I wake. My old bones are fatigued. Much has happened in the last few days. The sands of time have been kind to me – until now. I feel my energy depleting. Must I leave Devil's End without passing on the grimoire, or my knowledge? The thought makes me feel uncharacteristically low. Death holds no fear for me, but leaving Devil's End unguarded does.

It is a dark day, one that reflects my mood. The atmosphere is humid. The temperature suggests that a storm is coming that will put an end to summer and herald in the autumn. I don't relish the idea of another cold winter. Yes – I'm weary.

I walk downstairs. The house feels cool. Pottering in the kitchen for a while I put away the washed and dried pots in the cupboard. I straighten my tea towels over the rail and I look around the room as though believing this is for the last time.

When I'm gone, someone else will buy this house and modernise it. Perhaps have one of those dishwashing machines. I'd considered it myself once …

This thought makes me reflective. The house needs improvement. It needs to be modernised. It needs a new keeper that can revitalise it. Happiness should return to these walls and, perhaps too, the laughter of the young.

I take a cup of tea into the lounge and sit in my armchair, pulling a blanket over my legs. I'm colder than I should be for this time of year, and I think about lighting the fire, but that feels as though I'm accepting the onslaught of winter too soon.

The grimoire lies in its usual place on the table beside my chair. I reach for it. Running my hands over the worn leather, but it no longer reacts to me the way it should. The leather is cold: usually I feel a warm tingle on my finger tips, and a feeling of wellbeing, a sense that it belongs to me. But not today.

What has changed?

I sigh.

'The time is near then, it can no longer be held back?' I say. The grimoire glows once then the light and warmth dies.

I sit back in my chair. Pick up my tea and drink. The drink is the best I have ever had. When the cup is drained, I push aside the blanket and stand. I need to touch my crystal ball, the silver box containing Victor's ashes and my bag of runes. I need to say goodbye to all that is mine. I'm not usually so sentiment.

'What will you tell me now?' I say but I don't look into the crystal ball, nor do I cast the runes. I don't need to see what is coming – I know already.

My hand gently holds the ankh pendant around my neck. My touchstone and friend for more years than I care to say. On instinct I remove it and place it on the table beside my empty cup.

A sound outside – a pattern of musical notes – leaks into my thoughts with the persistence of an earworm. The music is familiar and I become aware once more of the world beyond my home. I have heard this before, a long time ago but the recollection of when escapes me. Then, that feeling of *déjà vu* returns and with it a sense of unreality, as though I'm already disconnecting with my body. As though my astral form is ready to flee this mortal and increasingly limiting and binding prison.

Yes I *have* heard this before. But when? Why now? Why is important that my aged brain should remember?

The door opens behind me, and before I turn to see who has entered, I remember when I last felt this way. It was the day I met Lobelia, and my inheritance was received. More importantly it was the day my sister, Poppy, disappeared. We never learnt what had happened to her … Perfume. *Lily of the Valley.* I am rooted to the spot, too afraid to hope. My senses have never been so heightened.

'Olive?'

I would know that voice anywhere. I force myself to turn. The effort is exhausting.

Poppy stands before me. She is exactly as she was the night she vanished so long ago. Not a day older! She is a young and attractive woman. Dark haired, flashing energetic eyes: she looks as I once did in my youth. Except ... I never wore pigtails.

'Poppy? Where have you been?' I say.

I cannot take my eyes from her lovely face. She is in every detail just as she was the day she disappeared. She is even wearing the same clothing.

'Time has not moved in the same way for me,' she explains.

I see images floating in her glowing white aura: a purity of colour that I've not seen around anyone else. She is untainted by the world. How is this possible unless she had not lived in it?

Magic floats around her: I see worlds beyond my comprehension. They live in her memory. She *has* changed! *But all for the better*. Poppy has the knowledge already needed to take care of things here.

'You have done so much to protect Devil's End,' she says.

'Oh Poppy!' I say. 'It's really you!'

'Yes, Olive. And I have come to take away your burden, and fulfil my destiny.'

She looks at the grimoire and it glows, it hurts my eyes. It is not the familiar yellow light which shone for me, but a bright white. I lift it and hold it out to Poppy.

I want to say, *Take this, and with it all of my memories, all of the knowledge needed to protect this place and this world* but the words won't come.

Poppy looks down at the grimoire and then she carefully takes it from my hands.

'I love you,' she says.

'I love you too ...'

I sink down into my chair. The feeling of unreality grows, but suddenly I'm free. I turn and see my old body, sitting in the chair, eyes closed. Poppy places a kiss on my forehead.

I feel no fear.

The mantle is passed and a new guardian installed. And now that I am free of the limiting mortal coil, I understand where she has been, and why this had to be so. For the universe is eternal, but there can be no escape from destiny.

Hawthorne witches have warded off evil for centuries, and they will continue to do so now that Poppy has been returned.

'Sleep well,' she says holding my hand. 'Dear sister. It is time for you to rest. Devil's End will remain in Hawthorne hands and you need not worry anymore. I accept the burden.'

I don't feel her touch but know my magic will live on in her.

I hear that music again. It is clearer this time: this is a melody played only for me.

It is my time to fly from this world.

Poppy leaves my still body and hurries to the door as though she feels my spirit leaving.

The light intensifies. It burns my ethereal eyes. My spirit drifts away, following the light, through time and space and other worlds and dimensions. *The supernatural is everywhere.*

I see Poppy in the distance now, leaving the cottage, my grimoire clasped tightly in her arms. It glows, but not as brightly as the light ahead.

'Fight on,' I call, though I know she cannot see or hear me.

I turn once again, the light awaits, and I follow knowing it will lead me to my eternal peace.

'Come Olive,' a kind voice says. 'Devil's End is in safe hands.'

DOSSIER
Andrew-Mark Thompson

On the following pages are various artifacts which have been collected over time. These have been smuggled out from the UNIT archives at great personal expense and danger by Andrew-Mark Thompson and are presented here as an addendum to this text, and perhaps as a warning for the future.

A confiscated image taken of one of the strange explosions at the Church of St Michael's in Devil's End.

Of course the newspapers and magazines had a field day with the story. This is a somewhat sensationalised cover from *Fortean Mail*.

WILTSHIRE Gazette
and HERALD

PICTURES FROM MISS SATANHALL CONTEST

FULL REPORT on page 5

Every Thursday   Edition 4987   Week ending 5th May 19

HUGE EXPLOSION TEARS THROUGH LOCAL CHURCH

MANY FEARED DEAD FOLLOWING MAJOR INCIDENT AT VILLAGE

A huge explosion has destroyed the picturesque church at Devil's End resulting in a number of fatalities.

The victims are thought to include the acting vicar of the parish and a number of well-known village dignitaries. The authorities have yet to release the names of the dead.

A statement by the police said that the explosion was thought to be caused by a build up of marsh gases in the church's crypt as a result of an excavation of the ancient burial site at the Devil's Hump less than a mile away.

LIVE BROADCAST

A similar release of gases is also believed to be behind the disruption of the BBC's live broadcast of the dig, the previous night.

Following the explosion, villagers were assisted in rescue attempts by army soldiers who were in the area on manuevers. They cordened off the area and were supported by a helicopter. Early reports suggested that the helicopter may have crashed but this has yet to be substantiated.

A spokesman for the army group, Captain Michael Yates stated that the area was potentially still dangerous and that sightseers should stay away until further notice. "We cannot guarantee that there will not be more explosions and for that reason, Devil's End remains a quarantined area for all members of the public. We are evacuating the local inhabitants to a safe area and from there they will be looked after and debriefed." He added.

Due to the evacuation, witnesses are difficult to come by but one, who wished to remain anonymous said that the incident ocurred on the Monday afternoon around 2pm during the village's annual Mayday celebrations.

He went on to tell our reporter, "The village green was full of people dancing round the maypole. Kids eating ice creams. Lots of music. Suddenly, some men in monks' habits came running from the church screaming.

"Then the whole thing went up in a huge flash of smoke and debris. It was strange that following the explosion everyone carried on as normal.

"They must've thought that it was part of the fun as most of them went back to the pub for a pint... especially the army blokes. Which surprised me..."

There has yet to be any formal statement from local authorites other than a brief release stating that the situation is "under control."

The BBC has stated that its live broadcast from the Devil's Hump had concluded well before the incident and that its presenter - the popular reporter Alistair Fergus - is safe but shaken by the news.

Further coverage is on pages 3, 4 and 8.

SPORTS NEWS	page 18
TV LISTINGS	page 9
LOCAL WEATHER	page 3

A more traditional piece of reporting from the *Wiltshire Gazette*. Here the cover story prepared by UNIT is given ...

A photograph snapped by one of the locals of a sign placed on the door to the cavern under the church.

After the church was destroyed, investigations took place into who had created the small, apparently stone, creature which was seen by many running about. This business card was found in the Cavern.

A historic flier promoting the May Day celebrations in Devil's End.

The *Radio Times* cover for the week. Gilbert Horner's investigation of the Devil's Hump was extensively promoted, despite the fact that it all seemed at first to be a publicity gimmick for his new book. His publicists later ended up as advisers to the UK government.

PAGE 23

BBC 3

Daring action reporter Alistair Fergus is live in Wiltshire at 11.45

11.15
Two Pints of Mild and a Packet of Pork Scratchings
Comedy situation drama
Producer GLENVILLE CAKE
Directed by RAMPTON HUNGE
Rpt

11.45
The Passing Parade Live from Devil's End

Presented by **Alistair Fergus**
Live coverage of the opening of the Devil's Hump barrow in Wiltshire. At midnight **Professor Jack Horner** and his team of archaeologists will be taking their first look inside the ancient burial mound and discovering the secrets of pagan man. What will they find? And will the curse manifest itself? With live comment from the Passing Parade team in the studio lead by **Michael Parkinson**
Location Producer HARRY HILLOCK
Production Team BRUCE HUMBLE, SIMON MALLOY
ROY OLIVER, SONNIE WILLS

12.30am
Epilogue
Read by **Peter Wyngarde**
Producer ARLO STANCE

12.35
Closedown

Cutting from the *Radio Times* for BBC3's transmission of Gilbert Horner opening the ancient Barrow, the Devil's Hump.

The cover of Horner's book. Following the events televised live, it became an instant bestseller, rivalling *Chariots of the Gods* by Erich von Daniken. Its popularity was helped by the fact that, following the live broadcast from Devil's End, during which Horner lost his life, the BBC cancelled the rest of his series.

The back cover of Horner's book.

Who were the Pagan Britons
that inhabited the British Isles
at the dawn of recorded
history?

In this new book, based on
the popular BBCtv series,
Prof. GILBERT HORNER digs
into the mysteries of our
ancient ancestors.

From the burial mounds of
Nuton Hoo to the great
archaeological digs of
Lake Vortigen in Carbury,
Prof. Horner takes the reader
on a journey into unknown
history and the depths of
pagan man.

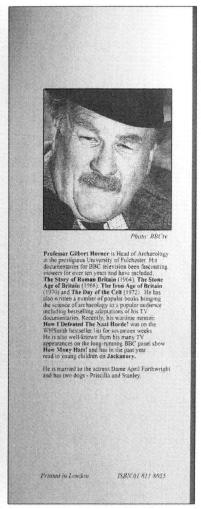

Photo: BBCtv

Professor Gilbert Horner is Head of Archaeology
at the prestigious University of Fulchester. His
documentaries for BBC television been fascinating
viewers for over ten years and have included:
The Story of Roman Britain (1964), **The Stone
Age of Britain** (1968), **The Iron Age of Britain**
(1970) and **The Day of the Celt** (1972). He has
also written a number of popular books bringing
the science of archaeology to a popular audience
including bestselling adaptations of his TV
documentaries. Recently, his wartime memoir
How I Defeated The Nazi Horde! was on the
WHSmith bestseller list for seventeen weeks.
He is also well-known from his many TV
appearances on the long-running BBC panel show
How Many Hats! and has in the past year
read to young children on **Jackanory**.

He is married to the actress Dame April Forthwright
and has two dogs - Priscilla and Stanley.

£1.50

Printed in London   *ISBN 01-811 8055*

The fly-leaf information from Horner's book.

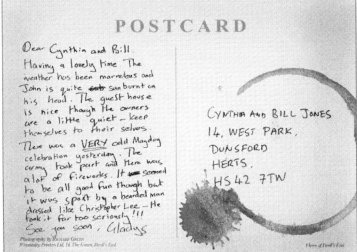

Among the artifacts is this postcard sent from Devil's End shortly after the May Day celebrations. It is not known who 'Gladys' or 'Cynthia and Bill Jones' are. The postcard was never sent.

AFTERWORD
Keith Barnfather

White Witch of Devil's End was a long time in the making. Originally mooted after Anastasia (my business partner and wife) and I had interviewed Damaris Hayman for our ongoing *Myth Makers* documentary series.

We were both amazed at her zest for life and hunger to act again, even in her early 80s, and we set about putting some ideas in motion …

That was in 2010 … yes, it's taken that long to go from those early thoughts to finally getting the drama completed.

During that time, Damaris has been incredibly supportive and understanding. Sam, David and all the writers have waited patiently … and Anastasia and I have got married (twice) and had a marvellous baby boy … Charalambos (Harry).

When, earlier this year, Koch Media asked if Reeltime had a new television drama we could release at Christmas, completing *White Witch of Devil's End* became a priority and the idea of putting it into a special box set with *Return to Devil's End* (our documentary about the filming of *The Dæmons*) was born.

The Dæmons of Devil's End was the result and as you read this it should just about be 'hitting the street'!

During one of the many, and I do mean many, long conversations I've had with David and Sam this year, I voiced a passing thought that it would be lovely if they considered publishing a novelisation of their scripts … little did I realise that this marvellous compendium would be the result! This is far more than just a novelisation … it's a development of the concepts behind *White Witch of Devil's End* into something more, that is only possible using the written word.

AFTERWORD

So calling this tome *The Dæmons of Devil's End* seemed entirely appropriate and I commend it to you and hope you have (or will) enjoy it as much as we all have enjoyed our part in making it happen. My grateful thanks to Sam, David and the authors.

Finally, if I may be so bold, I'd like to dedicate this book to Damaris Hayman ... one of the most talented actors I have ever worked with and an amazing person, whose indomitable spirit matches that of Olive Hawthorne's ... in fact there were a few times filming I almost lost myself in the world she wove around us!

This one's for you Damaris ... with my deepest love and respect.

Keith Barnfather
October 2017

ABOUT THE AUTHORS

PROLOGUE, THE INHERITANCE, EPILOGUE
Horror and Fantasy writer **Sam Stone** is the author of 15 novels (Including *The Vampire Gene Series*, *The Jinx Chronicles*), five novellas (*The Kat lightfoot Mysteries Series*, *The Darkness Within*), two horror collections (*Zombies in New York and Other Bloody Jottings*, *Cthulhu and Other Monsters*) and over 40 short stories. She has since expanded her writing credits to audio, stage and screen. Stone's works can be found in paperback, audio, screen and e-book and she is the commissioning editor of Telos Publishing's Moonrise imprints.
www.sam-stone.com

HALF LIGHT
Writer and musician **Suzanne Barbieri**'s first published written work was an analysis of the mythological and occult themes of the work of Clive Barker entitled *Clive Barker: Mythmaker for the Millennium*, which was published by the British Fantasy Society. Since then she has had numerous short stories published, including 'Its Secret Diary' which was nominated for a BSFA (British Science Fiction Association) award. As a singer and musician she has provided vocals for many artists and companies, and also produces solo work under the project name of Beloved Aunt.
suzannebarbieri.wordpress.com

THE CAT WHO WALKED THROUGH WORLDS
Debbie Bennett tells lies and makes things up. Sometimes people pay her for it. She mostly writes dark and gritty crime thrillers and claims to get her inspiration from the day job – but

if she told you about that, she'd have to kill you afterwards.
www.debbiebennett.co.uk

THE POPPET

Jan Edwards is a Sussex-born writer now living in the West Midlands with her husband and obligatory cats. She was a Master Locksmith for twenty years but also tried her hand at bookselling, microfiche photography, livery stable work, motorcycle sales and market gardening. She is a practising Reiki Master. She won a Winchester Slim Volume prize and her short fiction can be found in crime, horror and fantasy anthologies in UK, US and Europe; including *The Mammoth Book of Dracula* and *The Mammoth Book of Moriarty*.
janedwardsblog.wordpress.com

DÆMOS RETURNS

David J Howe has been involved with *Doctor Who* research and writing for over thirty years. He wrote the book *Reflections: The Fantasy Art of Stephen Bradbury* for Dragon's World Publishers and has contributed short fiction to *Peeping Tom, Dark Asylum, Decalog, Dark Horizons, Kimota, Perfect Timing, Perfect Timing II, Missing Pieces, Shrouded by Darkness* and *Murky Depths*, and factual articles to *James Herbert: By Horror Haunted* and *The Radio Times Guide to Science Fiction*. Another notable work of fiction is *talespinning,* a collection containing David's many short story pieces and screenplays.
www.howeswho.co.uk

HAWTHORNE BLOOD

Raven Dane is an award-winning fantasy author whose published works include the highly acclaimed *Legacy of the Dark Kind* series of dark fantasy/sci-fi vampire crossover novels (*Blood Tears, Blood Lament* and *Blood Alliance*). Raven's skills in fiction don't end there: her comedy fantasy *The Unwise Woman of Fuggis Mire* – a scurrilous spoof of high fantasy clichés – was met with great enthusiasm by the reading public. In more recent years Raven has met with critical acclaim for her

steampunk/occult adventures *Cyrus Darian and the Technomicron* and *Cyrus Darian and the Ghastly Horde* which are being republished by Telos in their Moonrise imprint Steampunk Visions.
www.raven-dane.com

DOSSIER
Andrew-Mark Thompson is a freelance graphic designer based in Derby. At various points over the past few decade he has found employment as a shop assistant, actor, special effects designer, stuntman, writer, museum guide, radio presenter, puppeteer, dancer, call centre operator, cowboy, graphic designer, drop-in centre co-ordinator and theme park rides manager. He also edited and wrote for a handful of *Doctor Who* and cult TV fanzines during the '80s and '90s. He is currently one of the organisers of Whooverville, which takes place in Derby every year around September-ish. He is single and was recently adopted by a stray cat.
andydrewz64.blogspot.co.uk

Other Telos Titles

TANITH LEE
Blood 20
20 vampire stories through the ages

Death Of The Day
Standalone crime novel

Tanith Lee A-Z
An A-Z collection of short fiction by Tanith Lee (forthcoming)

GRAHAM MASTERTON
The Djinn
The Wells Of Hell
Rules of Duel (With William S Burroughs)

PAUL FINCH
Cape Wrath And The Hellion
Terror Tales Of Cornwall Ed. Paul Finch

KIT COX
Dr Tripps: Kaiju Cocktail
Steampunk romp

FREDA WARRINGTON
Nights Of Blood Wine
Vampire horror short story collection

STEPHEN LAWS
Spectre

RHYS HUGHES
Captains Stupendous

For more titles and information:

TELOS PUBLISHING
www.telos.co.uk

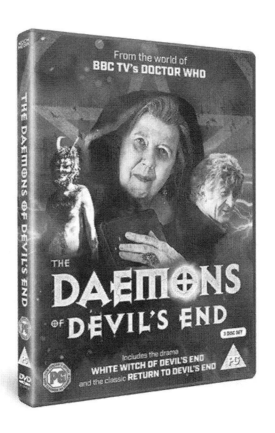

WATCH THE ORIGINAL DRAMA

AVAILABLE FROM AMAZON
AND ALL DVD RETAILERS.

www.timetraveltv.com

17833911R00100

Printed in Great Britain
by Amazon